THE INDUS CHALLENGE

Dr R. Durgadoss (his associates call him Dr DD) is an entrepreneur, inspirational speaker, writer and coach. He holds a PhD in Corporate Finance. He has a career spanning more than three decades with leading multinational institutions of high repute.

He has a deep-rooted passion for Indian mythology, history and philosophy. Since his childhood, he has been able to attract a number of followers with his mesmerizing storytelling abilities. Wherever history is a mystery, he fills gaps with his creative spin.

Having held his audience spellbound with powerful storytelling during his lectures in international forums, he thought it was time to focus on a series of fiction in the historical/mythological genre. *The Indus Challenge* is the second book in this series.

Facebook: http://www.facebook.com/DrDurgadoss
Twitter: https://twitter.com/DrDurgadoss
Website: http://www.drdd.co.in
Youtube: https://www.youtube.com/user/DurgadossAiyer

Also by the author:

Fiction
A Saint in the Boardroom
The Shackles of the Warrior [Janam One]

THE INDUS CHALLENGE

R. DURGADOSS

RUPA

Published by
Rupa Publications India Pvt. Ltd 2016
7/16, Ansari Road, Daryaganj
New Delhi 110002

Sales centres:
Allahabad Bengaluru Chennai
Hyderabad Jaipur Kathmandu
Kolkata Mumbai

This is a work of fiction. Names, characters, places and incidents
are either the product of the author's imagination or are used
fictitiously and any resemblance to any actual person, living or dead,
events or locales is entirely coincidental and is not intended to hurt any
segment of our society. The author does not claim the accuracy of the
mythological/historical information used in this work.

While every effort has been made to trace copyright holders and
obtain permission, this has not been possible in all cases; any
omissions brought to our attention will be remedied in future editions.

ISBN: 978-81-291-4498-0

First impression 2016

10 9 8 7 6 5 4 3 2 1

The moral right of the author has been asserted.

Printed by HT Media Ltd, Noida

Dedicated to the Almighty

CONTENTS

Introduction: Janam Two	ix
Prologue	xxi
Part I: Freedom at Midnight	1
Part II: Sweetheart : Sour Thoughts	25
Part III: The Confession of a Greek Princess	35
Part IV: Rudra Recalls	93
Part V: The Grand Hunt	117
Part VI: Samrat Speaks	179
Part VII: Back to Pataliputra	199
Part VIII: The Indo-Greek Matrimony	215
Part IX: The Tragedy Struck	241
Part X: The Unresolved Puzzle	251
Part XI: The Mysterious Murder	261
Part XII: The Turning Point	267
Epilogue	277
Acknowledgements	285
Glossary	287
Bibliography	291

Introduction: Janam Two

Recap...
Track Travelled So Far...
Janam One: The Shackles of the Warrior

2008 AD

A terrorist group attacks the world by planting viruses into global computer systems through a satellite orbiting the earth. This act of cyber terrorism disrupts air traffic systems, interferes with the control system for water and electricity, blocks commercial communications, crashes various network systems, gains access to secret military information and defaces websites. In light of this cyber attack, the world is facing a chaotic situation.

Shiv, a young, celebrated NASA scientist destroys the group's moves and saves the earth from cyber attacks. To honour Shiv's extraordinary performance, a felicitation function was held at Taj Mahal Palace Hotel, Mumbai, on the fateful day of 26th November 2008. Shiv, the cyber warrior, becomes a victim of a physical terrorist attack at the Taj Mahal. His mind flashes with several images while he lies in a coma in the ICU of a leading hospital in Mumbai. The images of war, weapons and weeping widows swamp his mind. Are these flashes from his previous births?

3000 BC

The heroes who saved the planet from cyber terrorists could not avoid succumbing to this physical terrorism. Why? Why? This is what Shiv's unconscious mind questioned.

The memories from his time in a coma were inexplicable. They were like a patchwork quilt, with no apparent sequence nor temporal relationship to one another. The purest and the most extraordinary part of his journey had commenced deep in his state of coma. In the midst of his coma, his cerebrum unleashed a quest to unravel his past. Then all of a sudden, everything opened up. His mind entered a valley, so crisp and beautiful that he could see with clarity.

He could see waterfalls, pools of water, and indescribable colours with arcs of silver and gold light and beautiful hymns emanating from them. Boom! Suddenly, the serene image shifted into images of war, weapons and weeping widows. He saw himself on the mast of a tall ship, he saw himself in a missile silo, and he saw himself on the watchtower of a mammoth fort, and then guiding the cannons of a great warship. And then he saw images of himself move out of the earth and out of the universe. He had lost awareness of his physical body during his coma. In the process of this search, his mind realized many of his previous states, breaking the shackles of all his earlier births.

His mind was filled with the chorus of a great army crying out the name, 'Sagar, Sagar, Sagar....' He was lying on the battlefield, a wounded solider covered with deep cuts. It was a bloodbath all around.

He was holding back his last breath, waiting for his beloved wife and newly born son. It was the battle between the Kauravas and Pandavas, in the land situated between the two rivers, the Sarasvati and Drishadvati, the land where Manu wrote his *Manu-smriti* and the land where the *Rig* and *Sama Vedas* were compiled.

His calm mind resisted the image. 'This battleground is not the land of my birth or my beloved kingdom. This is not the place where I spent my joyful childhood. This is not the beautiful place where I come from. I need to find the place of my birth.'

His comatose mind continued to wander further into the past. It now flashed images of the spectacular city of his birth. The golden fort of this city threw its yellow glitter on the surrounding waters, making it look like flames were rising from the riverbed. There was a township with six sectors along the banks of the river. It was connected to the mainland via floating bridges, which could be withdrawn whenever there was an attack. The floating bridges and the design of the city were truly marvellous.

Having identified the city of his birth, he stumbled onto his colourful life as 'Sagar', the great warrior of the kingdom of Krishna in 3083 BC!

Sagar, in his first karmic avatar, was given the 'Shudra varna' tag but was patronized by a Brahmin guru. He was given the status of a Shudra by society but the status of a strategic warrior by his leader, Abhimanyu. He grew up with three Brahmin friends (the sons of his Guruji), the Kshatriya leader Abhimanyu and another friend, a Vaishya. A close bond developed between them in the gurukul. The three sons of his Guruji were also blessed with mystic powers.

All the *Pancha bhoodas*—earth, water, sky, air and fire— danced to the tunes of the three boys who had been born as triplets to his Guruji. They were all more or less the same age as him.

One boy was extraordinarily proficient in earth-related matters. He knew the topography, water bodies, likelihood of an earthquake, how to create tremors in the earth. He could identify the movement of the creatures beneath the ground. He could create a hole, go into the earth and come out at another place by navigating below the surface. He could stay beneath the earth for months without anyone knowing of it. When he fought on earth, no one could conquer him.

The second boy was blessed with extraordinary powers in water. He could swim below the water, stay inside it for ages, invoke *Varuna* and bring rain at will. When he fought on water, no one could conquer him.

The third boy was highly talented in matters of the sky. He could invoke the *Vayu* (air), change the direction of the wind, speak to the birds, talk to people in a far-off place through the air. When he fought from a height, no one could defeat him.

Only when the three were together would the *Pancha bhoodas* obey them. They were warned of a threat to their lives at the age of fifteen. As they grew older, they joined Abhimanyu's 'Yuva Warrior Team'.

Sagar was the chief strategist of the Yuva army, marshalling resources for his leader Abhimanyu. During the Kuru war, on Yuva Sena, the fateful day of the chakravyuha, Sagar had been advised by his Guruji that he should not send his three gifted sons to the field. According to their horoscopes, their lives were under threat.

But fate took the decision away from him.

A nine-layer chakravyuha had been formed by Guru Drona. All of Duryodana's greatest warriors were in the inner circle, while the outer circle was protected by the mighty Drona. The Pandava warrior Arjuna, the only one who knew

↑ Chakravyuha entrance

how to cleave the chakravyuha, had been dragged off to a different field. Now the onus of breaking the chakravyuha fell to the young Abhimanyu, Arjuna's son. He knew how to break the chakravyuha; he did not know how to exit it.

The Yuva Sena headed by Abhimanyu volunteered to enter the chakravyuha, assigning the seniors the task of ensuring that the breach remained open to allow for a clear line of retreat. A contingency plan was made.

The three Brahmin boys' powers would be used to create an underground tunnel through each tier, so that the soldiers would be able to retreat in case anything went wrong. A portion of the army could also use the tunnels so that they could be shielded from arrows while moving ahead and defending the broken edges of the tier. Also, even if the tiers were closed due to any reason, the mouths of the tunnels would provide a ready exit for Abhimanyu.

The innovative tactic of outsmarting the chakravyuha by using the mystical powers of the Sena brothers was deliberated upon in the strategy discussions held in the early meetings.

When the Yuva Sena was ready to enter the chakravyuha, one of the southern kings supporting the Pandavas thundered:

'How do you expect my forces to be lead by a Shudra? It's not possible. I will not allow this.'

Abhimanyu and Sagar were hurt and knew that time was being wasted. The arrangement of forces to counter the chakravyuha would take at least half a *nazhiga* (One nazhiga equals 24 minutes as a day divided into 60 nazhigas). Abhimanyu asked Sagar to stay silent and stated that he would explain the situation. But no one was listening to him. As the talks went on between Abhimanyu and the southern kings, an emissary arrived with a message stating that Sagar's wife had given birth to a baby boy.

Abhimanyu wanted Sagar to go and be with his wife, see his son and come back. In the meantime, he would make the arrangements for the army. But the southern kings were adamant. They would not fight under a Shudra. Exasperated, Abhimanyu and Sagar gave up. Abhimanyu instructed Sagar to go back and be with his wife. He asked one of the southern kings to be the rearguard instead.

Sagar said to Abhimanyu, 'I do not know whether to be happy for my son or sad that on the eve of battle, I cannot be with you.'

Abhimanyu replied, 'Keep the sweets ready. I will come back and we will celebrate the birth of your son.'

Sagar went to his Brahmin friends. 'You should be very careful. Stay with Abhimanyu at all times. So long as you are with Abhimanyu, I will not be afraid. Also, under no circumstances should you get separated. Stay together and ride together.'

Sagar moved off of battlefield with a guilty feeling, afraid that he was leaving the three boys and foregoing his Guruji's strict instructions.

In the meantime, Abhimanyu's young blood and the heat of the battle overtook him. He fought alone, like a warrior who does not value his own life. He started to move further ahead, while his army, which could not match his swiftness, began to fall back. All his uncles were stuck far behind near the first tier of the chakravyuha.

His rearguard was pursued and attacked by Drona. The three Brahmin boys with special powers were separated in the melee which took place. Since they were separated, they could not invoke the *Pancha bhoodas*. Their mystic skill only worked when they were together. Plans for the tunnel were turned to dust and with them went the last ray of hope for a safe return.

Moreover, the strategic master, Sagar, who channelized their mystic powers into a coordinated strategy, was not there with them. Hence, each one of them became a powerless island, lending no assistance with their supernatural abilities.

The senior Pandavas were held back at the entrance of the chakravyuha, while the circles of the chakravyuha were closed by their opponents, leaving the Yuva Sena boys—Abhimanyu and the three Brahmin boys—struck inside different tiers. After a valiant battle, the soul of the young hero Abhimanyu departed this world, unsatisfied. He had bravely fought to the best of his abilities. Had his opponents been honourable, and if he had more time, he would have surely destroyed all of them. Drona was satisfied, as he had struck a blow that would hurt the Pandavas. The chakravyuha had served its purpose.

Among the thousands who died on that day were the three Brahmin boys. Not being able to evoke their mystical powers, they lay dead in different tiers within the chakravyuha.

Sagar had been betrayed by his Vaishya wife. She had married him while pretending to love him, while in fact she desired to take revenge on him thinking that his Shudra father had been the cause of her father's death. She had unveiled their secret plan for the chakravyuha to the enemy, which brought complete havoc on the Yuva Sena warriors—including Abimanyu and the three Brahmin boys.

Sagar spoke of the tragedy to his Guruji, who was meditating across the river. He roared, 'Sagar, I told you not to send my three sons to the war, as they had to suffer from a life threat at the age of fifteen. You promised to protect them. You are responsible for this. You knew they were blessed children. They were supposed to be extraordinary warriors on land, sea and air, supported by all the *Pancha bhoodas*. You shortened their lives. They might have lived at least three times longer. The story of their lives will always be that of success, and incompleteness. You have nipped their lives in the bud by not sticking to your word.

'I hereby curse you. You will live the forty-five years of each of my sons' remaining lives. But you will not live it in full. You will have the capability of each of my sons and like them, you will also die at the age of fifteen. Thus, you will take three births for each of my sons. You will take nine incarnations after this birth.

'You will be highly competent on land, sea and air matters in each of the three births. You can win a war but you cannot avail the fruits of it. Let these nine births forever remind you that you killed my sons in the nine-tier chakravyuha. Each of the nine circles will represent one birth for you. This is my curse. And yet, my anger is not slaked.'

Sagar was stunned. He could not understand how the fate could turn around so. His Guru, the one who had almost adopted him, who was equal to his own father and had been everything to him, had turned against him.

'He is a true Brahmin, and his curse will force me to face miseries in my subsequent births,' he thought.

He pleaded with his Guru, saying that he was not the only cause behind the death of his sons. He explained how circumstances such as the birth of his son and the revolt of the southern kings had prohibited him from participating in the battle on that day. But Guruji did not reply to him, did not bother to listen to him and turned away.

Later, as he lay on his death bed the next day, Sagar learned the secrets of his birth in a Kshatriya family and also about the betrayal of his wife.

He pleaded with his Guruji on his death bed.

'Guruji,

- I was penalized as a low caste Shudra even though I was a born Kshatriya.
- I was penalized by my wife for a cause to which I and my family were not a party.
- I was penalized by you for the death of your sons for which I was not the cause.

'I do not know why I have been singled out by my fate and punished for no fault of mine. But, I will not curse my fate, I lived true to the people around me, I was passionate in whatever I was doing, and I am willing to accept the result as they unfold. I truly believe that I have had to chase my goals but the same time, I have had to learn to face the results. My only wish is that no one on earth be denied opportunities on grounds of his caste, creed or colour.

'Life may crown a person or make him a beggar on the streets. But no one should deprive anyone else of opportunities. Everyone should have equal opportunities. From below the ground comes a diamond, from the mud comes the lotus. Greatness can come from anyone. A mother's womb should not determine one's destiny. I am saying this after facing troubles from the womb to my tomb. This is my death wish, Guruji,' Sagar concluded.

Bharadwaj had tears in his eyes, 'My dear Sagar, you speak like a philosopher. You have matured beyond your age. In the philosophy sessions at the gurukul, I saw the sparks in you. Today I am seeing those sparks flare into flames. I have to correct myself. I gave you a curse of having a short life in your nine future births.

'I cannot take back my curse, and the arrow once out of the bow cannot be retrieved. I have no powers to withdraw it, but I can soften the curse. For each of the nine births to follow, I double your years from fifteen to thirty in each of the nine births. That is the best I can do, Sagar. But in every one of your births you will have a great impact on society. In three of your births, you will have special powers regarding land, the next three you will have special powers over water and next three you will have special powers over air. Had my sons lived they would have excelled in land, water and air.'

Turning to Sagar's wife, Bharadwaj said, 'You lived a false life with Sagar, even though he gave you pure love. For cheating him like this, you will continuously beg for his help as a prisoner of war in your next birth. You will meet your husband, and he will be the army chief and save you from prison. You have the chance to break your own chakras of rebirth when you sincerely love your husband in the next birth.'

A new journey was about to begin for these two souls. The soul of Varsha would next be a prisoner of war, begging and pleading for support from the soul of Sagar. Where would this meeting take place? What sort of people would they be at their next outing?

The Indus Challenge: Janam Two

The hero, Rudra, was born in 330 BC with a new karmic agenda. Would he be able to break the shackles of destiny and overcome the curse...?

Prologue

330 BC

The Macedonians and Greeks came with Alexander the Great to the Hindu Kush range. They were mesmerized by the land of the gods, snow-covered, forested mountains higher than Olympus. The sun rising and setting among the glistening peaks painted a breathtaking picture. They were entranced by the stories of the magical kingdoms of the air; of the heavens; of Vishnu and Shiva; of cities in the sky inhabited by sky demons. They were fascinated by the story of Surya, the sun god, who galloped across the sky each day in his golden chariot, pulled by the five horses, while down below in the dark bowels of the earth were giant serpents, red-eyed, flesh-eating demons and other creatures of the underworld.

It was at this time that the people of Bharat were looking inwards, while the Macedonians aggressively explored outwards and wanted to conquer the world. The kingdoms of Bharat were threatened by the aggressive Macedonians. No king or kingdom was free from the aggressor's attack. Fragmented kingdoms, disunity and distrust among the rulers made these kingdoms an easy target for the Macedonians.

During this period, several events are shrouded in mystery—what brought Alexander to India? How did he die at such a young age? What were the origins of Chandragupta Maurya? How did a young lad of humble origins take on a mighty king? How did a poor Brahmin pundit help a poor young man rise to power from nowhere? What extraordinary powers did Chandragupta possess that made him so successful? Who were his key generals? Who won wars for him? The questions are endless.

There are several seemingly unconnected dots, as the history of this time is shrouded in deep mystery. Rudra effortlessly unlocks the ancient secrets and aligns the unconnected dots. Mystery unravelled; secrets decoded...

In the second avatar (Janam Two) as Rudra during the tumultuous times of Alexander and Chanakya, he offers stunning clues and revelations. His decrypting skills leave a trail that answers several mysteries in our rich history.

At last, Rudra, heading the Nine Unknown Men Army (NUM), has arrived to decode the secrets to save humanity from cataclysm and extinction.

PART I

Freedom at Midnight

1

Parthiva year, 306 BC, Kartika (November) month, Friday evening.

The Massaga fort in the Hindu Kush had surrendered to Rudra, the commander-in-chief of the Mauryan army. He was taking stock of the situation. At this hour, a cry hit his ears. *'Meri raksha karo!* (Please save me from the barbarians!') A woman's shrieking voice reverberated against the mountains.

'Why does this lady cry so?' asked Rudra, looking curiously at his companion. He turned in the direction from where the voice was coming. To his surprise, he saw two cages in which two persons stood, chained. There was a young woman around twenty-two years old, and in the other cage was a bright young lad.

Rudra looked at the cage closely. The woman was gorgeous, seductive, shapely. Her hair was kohl-black, and cascaded over her shoulders. She had thin eyebrows, velvety eyelashes, sea-nymph ears, a sharp nose, shiny white teeth, almond-shaped eyes and glossy skin.

She was wasp-waisted, and her pouting, luscious lips conveyed her displeasure. Her hips and bust were almost of equal size. Her perfect shape reminded him of many icons of beauty he had seen. Her fleshy rounded back attracted his attention.

Rudra realized that he was going overboard ogling at the young women. But in spite of her beautiful features, she seemed to be a fading flower, possibly due to her weakness and exhaustion.

He turned his head towards the surrendered commander of the opposing army, Dharma Sena.

'Dharma Sena, who are these caged persons?' asked Rudra.

'Forget these idiots, Commander. Let me take you round the fort.' Dharma Sena said, 'This is Massaga, the great fort city of the Asvakas, the tribe of horsemen. To the south and west are gigantic rocks which defy climbing. To the east is the swift-flowing mountain torrent, the Masakavati river. This famous fort is situated on a hill 6,000 feet high and has a circumference of twelve miles. At the top of the fort, there is arable land requiring a thousand men to cultivate it. This land is capable of feeding more than 30,000 men indefinitely. There are also perennial springs and reservoirs. Every hill here is a natural fort, Commander. Every man here is a horse soldier, Commander. A mighty rampart of stone, brick and timber surrounds the fort, which also has a moat on three sides and the river on the fourth.

'Commander, "Masika" means "serpent's hole", a name indicating the supposed impregnability of the fort and the valour of its defender.'

'I realize how impregnable your fort is, Dharma Sena. I had to use my best skills to tame you and your fort. By the way, I am impressed by the seven gates leading to the citadel. Can you give me an overview of your fort, Dharma Sena?'

'You have sharp eyes, Commander. You noticed our seven gates? I am impressed. Let me show you around.'

2

'The approach to your fort is a zigzag ascent rising for more than a mile from the plains. It was difficult terrain to cross, Dharma Sena,' said Rudra.

'In spite of the hindrances, you have conquered us, Commander. The moment our Greek satrap Rodrigus heard of your entry into the fort, he ran away with 5,000 Macedonian and barbarian soldiers. As a local representative of the people, I surrendered to you with the remaining soldiers. Your skills are amazing, Commander. You are an inspiring leader, one whose kind I have never seen in my lifetime.'

Rudra ignored the compliments of Dharma Sena. He was too seasoned to fall for superficial compliments, and preferred to observe a person's conduct over a period of time before coming to any conclusion about character.

The bridge to approach the fort spanned the river and was supported by ten arches, one of which had a curved shape. The rest were pointed. The ascending path passed through seven gateways. The seventh and final gate led directly into the palace, a complex that brought together a variety of residential and official structures.

All the gateways to the fort had been built as massive stone structures with secure fortifications for military defence. The doors of the gates with pointed arches were reinforced to fend off elephants and cannon shots. The top of the gates had notched parapets for archers to stand and shoot at the approaching army. A road within the fort linked all the gates and provided access to the numerous structures inside.

The naturally strong rock where the fort was located was further strengthened by the construction of embrasure walls and gateways. The citadel was located at the end of the seven gates and contained all the important buildings—meeting halls for the public, temples, granaries, marriage halls, stables, shrines, pavilions and prisons.

Rudra noticed that the roads inside the citadel were well laid out and had excellent paving. He did not fail to notice the massive drainage systems running through the entire citadel. The drainage openings were so tall that they could easily accommodate a person walking through them. Even a horseman could easily ride through such a tunnel on the back of his steed.

Impressed by this huge system, Rudra asked Dharma Sena, 'Are these underground passages? Where do they go?'

'Commander, these are drainage openings. The citadel is located in a plain surrounded by the mountains. Hence, water had to be removed from the plain by applying pressure. Therefore, we have created this massive drainage system at an incline. These underground tunnels are linked to the hill slopes. Again, we did not want the used water flowing down the slopes of the hill, so we closed these tunnels even on the hill slopes, in order to maintain aesthetics. In short, the water used in the citadel will ultimately reach the ground by moving downhill through these underground tunnels.'

'What are the sounds coming from these tunnels, Dharma Sena? Do you hear the hissing sounds? Are there any people working in these tunnels?'

'Commander, these are the sounds of the flowing water.

Nothing else,' replied Dharma Sena.

But Rudra felt the vibrations emanating from within; it sounded as though people were walking inside the underground tunnels. He made a mental note of it, but refrained from asking more questions.

'Commander, this fort represents the tribute to the nationalism, courage, chivalry and sacrifice of the erstwhile rulers before the takeover by the Macedonian satraps. Even the commoners, not just the rulers, consider death to be a better option than dishonour in the face of surrender to the foreign invaders. Today we have all surrendered to you, as you are an emissary from the ruler of Bharat, who is releasing us from the clutches of the barbarians. The day we surrendered to them is truly an unfortunate one in our history.'

'Dharma Sena, what were these unpleasant events you are referring to? Why did you surrender?'

'Commander, I will brief you upon reaching my office. Let us walk back to my office.'

3

While they were returning to the office, yet again the sound of the shrieking hit Rudra's ears. '*Meri raksha karo*! Please save me from the barbarians!'

'Dharma Sena. Who is this lady? Why is she caged? Why is she shouting?'

'Commander, I was just telling you a short while ago of some unpleasant events that happened in the past in our fort. This lady is one of the remnants of that time. Let me explain this to you, Commander. For the time being, please ignore her. Let us move to the office. Do not stand near that cage for too long. This lady is evil.'

'Go on, Dharma Sena, let me listen to your story.'

'Ashvajit, one of the greatest rulers in the land, was challenged by Dario, the Greek commander under Alexander. The Asvakas under Ashvajit drove the Greeks off after a fierce battle. Dario did not give up. A wooden tower was brought up against the wall and from here, the Greek archers shot at the Asvakas. Missiles were also discharged against the defenders. Ashvajit drew his men away, out of the range of these missiles. The Greeks were unable to force a way into the walls.

'The next day, Dario threw a bridge across the moat. A regiment of Macedonians rushed along the bridge which broke down under their weight and threw them into the water, where many were killed by the arrows, stones and other missiles thrown by the Asvakas. Many of the Greeks were wounded.

Dario told his deputy commander, "Unless we kill Ashvajit, the ruler, we cannot take this fort. Let us concentrate on him."

'The next day, the Macedonians hurled their missiles in hundreds at him. A chance missile struck him and Ashvajit fell, dead.

'The fort was stunned; the Asvakas were disheartened by the loss of their leader. At this point, the shameful thing happened.

'Avantika, the queen, asked the Asvakas not to fight. She met Dario with her young daughter and infant son and prayed to him to spare their lives. "Please spare my children," she pleaded with Dario.

'Dario was dazzled by her beauty. The Asvakas refused to give up. They said they would give up fighting only when their queen directed them to do so.

'Dario told the Asvakas that their queen was his prisoner. She would tell them to surrender. Weeping, she came out of Dario's tent, where she had been held. She asked her people to do as he said. They reluctantly obeyed their queen.

'That night, there was a banquet in the Greek camp and much drinking and singing followed. Avantika was also there as the new ally of the Macedonians. At the end of the revels she retired with Dario to his tent.

'Dario won many wars, but Avantika easily conquered him with her beauty.

'In the ancient custom of the Asvakas, a wife must commit sati on her husband's pyre. But carried away by her anxiety to save her young daughter and son, she sacrificed all that she had. What a nasty woman!

'Test a servant while in the discharge of his duty, a relative in difficulty, a friend in adultery and a wife in misfortune.

Ashvajit's wife, in the time of his people's misfortune, turned out to be a mistress of the barbarians. It is an insult to our pride.

'Beauty is spoiled by an immoral character. Avantika's beauty has fallen prey to her immoral attitude. A wicked wife, a false friend, a savvy servant and living in a house with a serpent in it mean nothing but death. Avantika is a wicked wife. This courtesan had forsaken her warrior husband. Untruthfulness, rashness, guile, stupidity, avarice, uncleanliness and cruelty are a bad woman's natural flaws. She has all these flaws.

'With her fell the Massaga fort and the Asvakas. Dario took over the fort. When he left along with Alexander, Rodrigus, the current satrap, was appointed in his place.'

'But tell me Dharma Sena—what have this caged woman and the boy to do with all this?'

'Commander, now I come to their connection to Avantika.'

4

'Commander, the caged girl is Swastika, and the blind boy is Visaka, her brother. Both are the children of Avantika, the queen who shamed us,' said Dharma Sena.

'What? Are they the children of the ruler? Why are they caged?'

'They are unfit to live in our land, Commander. They were sold to a Greek commander as slaves. They are ready to be dispatched to Athens,' said Dharma Sena.

'Why are you so angry, Dharma Sena?'

'Commander, they tried to poison me and kill me when I raised my voice against their mother's infidelity. These people had a bad upbringing.'

'Why did they try to kill you, Dharma Sena?'

'Commander, I was the second in command here, and represented the Asvaka tribes under Rodrigus. These children of the so-called royal lineage wanted to replace me and take my position.

'Not only that, having failed in their mission to poison me, the boy tried to stab me while I slept. My personal bodyguard grabbed him, and in the fight that followed, Visaka lost his eyes.

'This angered Rodrigus and he decided to send them to Athens as slaves. They were waiting to be deported and at this point, you captured our fort. Now we have to decide their fate, Commander.

'As a single withered tree, if set aflame, causes a whole

forest to burn, so do this son and daughter destroy the whole tribe. Hence they have to leave our land, Commander.'

'I hear you, Dharma Sena. What is next on the agenda?'

'Commander, I submit the Asvaka land to you and agree to come under Maurya rule with an annual payment to the Maurya kingdom. Please issue me the ordinance letter. After getting this letter, we will host a celebration for you.'

'That is good, Dharma Sena. Let me take our kingdom's mudhra and issue the letter right away.'

Saying this, Rudra began searching for his mudhra, but he could not find it.

'Dharma Sena, I seem to have lost my mudhra. Where did I...'

After a while, Rudra shouted, 'Ha! Dharma Sena, while we were talking near the cage where the young lady and lad were held, I left my mudhra there. Let me go there with my assistant. I will be back soon, don't worry.'

Saying this, Rudra started walking back to the cages where the two young royal prisoners were held.

5

Rudra and his team reached the cages in which Swastika and Visaka were held. Rudra went near the cage and his eyes scanned every inch of it.

Swastika came towards him and stood at the edge of the cage with only the iron bars separating her from Rudra. She looked at Rudra closely, into his eyes. Rudra was six feet tall and had a youthful appearance. He had an athletic body, symmetrical face, a narrow waist, a V-shaped torso and broad shoulders. 'His youthfulness, clear, smooth skin and the vivid colour of his eyes and hair must attract many beautiful women,' she thought.

Many thoughts crossed her mind. His slightly tanned skin blended well against his sandy blond hair. His wide brown eyes enhanced his elegance. 'I cannot help but stare at him,' she thought. 'He is truly the man of my dreams.' His smooth, spade-shaped beard and the bristly moustache gave an indication of his martial skills. He had a devil-may-care expression and a stellar smile. 'I can easily make out that he is the commander-in-chief of the Mauryan army which conquered the fort and stole it from the hands of the barbarians.'

'Did you see my mudhra here? I am sure I left it in the corner of this cage. Hey lady, I am asking you!' Rudra said to her.

His baritone voice matched his majestic masculinity.

'Please address me as Swastika, do not call me "lady". I

have a name,' she retorted.

'I know your name, Swastika. I heard your shrieking voice, asking everyone to save you. I have no time to waste. Did you see the mudhra I left here?'

'I know you are the commander-in-chief of the Mauryan army. The people around you shouted "Rudra, Rudra," when you conquered the fort. I know you left your mudhra here. I know our eyes met three times today. We were destined to meet, Commander. We seem to have a karmic bond. Do not ignore me on the advice of that treacherous Dharma Sena.

'He who befriends a man whose conduct is vicious, whose vision is impure and who is notoriously crooked is rapidly ruined. If you befriend Dharma Sena, the crook of this land, you will be doomed, Commander. The essence of strategy is what not to do, Commander. Please do not believe Dharma Sena's surrender shows meekness.

'Now will you save me and my brother from this barbarian? If you promise me that, I will give you your mudhra.'

'You are in no position to specify conditions. I have won so many battles. No one can tame me with their blackmail,' Rudra said.

'Commander, I will tell you a secret. If it is true, then you must release me and my brother,' she pleaded.

'Go on, what is the secret?' Rudra asked.

'The crook Dharma Sena might have given you an impression of surrender. He will invite you to a big celebration tonight. He is going to serve you poisoned food. He is planning to kill you. The moment you are dead, he is planning to call Rodrigus, who is hiding in the underground tunnels with 5,000 men from his army. Don't be trapped, Commander.'

'How did you know? You may be lying to me to get me

to help you.'

'No, Commander, this is true. I know the Greek language as I learnt it in my younger days with the help of my mother. Not knowing I could understand them, the Greek soldiers were talking about this near my cage, just before they went into their hideouts in the underground tunnels. In fact, 500 cavalrymen sitting on their horses are also hiding in the tunnels.

'See, Commander—is this your mudhra?' she took the mudhra from inside her blouse.

'Yes, Swastika, thank you, I did not want this mudhra to fall into the wrong hands. I will be careful in my dealings with Dharma Sena. If what you have said is true, I will demolish this army and release you unconditionally,' Rudra assured her. He took his mudhra and walked back to the palace for the late evening celebrations to be hosted by Dharma Sena.

6

Rudra reached the palace hall. He was received by Dharma Sena and his council of ministers. There was a festive mood all around. A few Greek faces could also be seen in the hall, the leftovers of the satrap's men.

The palace hall was a place of stunning beauty; the inner walls were covered with sheets of ornate metal.

Female musicians were present at the banquet. Dharma Sena, the present head of the palace led Rudra and his cohort to the sound of voices, flutes and pipes. Beautiful courtesans were keeping the guests enthralled with their performance.

The best of Greek wines were flowing freely in the hall. The barbarians had left all the wrong cultures behind them, Rudra thought. The culture of Bharat had to be brought back to its original reputation, erasing the traces of all these Greek vices.

The invasion of Greek culture was visible during the dinner. The table was filled with a wide variety of Greek wines, accompanied by snacks such as chestnuts, beans, toasted wheat and honey cakes, all intended to absorb the alcohol and extend the drinking spree.

With the exception of the courtesans, the banquet was restricted to allow only men.

A king of the banquet was drawn by lots. He had the task of directing the slaves on how strong the mix of the wine should be.

Rudra took a complete round of the hall. He was astonished

by the presentation of the dishes kept on the dinner table, waiting to be served.

Different kinds of bread, *mizithra* cheese, honey, soups, herbs, mashed beans, garlic, onions, fruit baskets filled with figs, pomegranates, mangoes, bananas and dried fruits were spread across the table.

Not only the main courses, but the astonishing varieties of desserts were also very impressive. But Rudra asked himself, was this dinner meant for the Greek satrap?

'Commander, can I give you some company?' A pleasing voice interrupted Rudra's thoughts. He turned in the direction of the voice.

He saw one of the most beautiful women he had ever laid eyes on. 'I am Apsara, the royal courtesan. I have been designated to entertain royal guests, Commander,' she said.

She took a glass of wine and served it to Rudra. 'Oh, Apsara, you are taking care of our commander. Today he is going to announce the annexation of Massaga under the rule of the Mauryas!' Dharma Sena announced.

Rudra politely declined her offer of wine, since he did not drink. However, he took a few nuts in order to honour his hosts. He was waiting for the appropriate moment to make his move.

After an hour of music and dance, he was seated at the royal table as the guest of honour along with the host, Dharma Sena. The soup was served. 'Commander, this is a herbal soup specially made for you. While the others are eating the other kinds of soup, the special soup was prepared just for you. Please start your dinner, Commander. You haven't touched the wine, but we will not let you miss out on any food.'

At this point, Dharma Sena's five-year-old son, Veer Sena,

came and sat on his father's lap.

Rudra did something which no one expected at that point of time. He drew Veer Sena to himself, and fed him the soup.

After drinking the soup, the boy fainted, fell down and foam began coming out of his mouth. Within minutes, he was dead.

The hall was silent. Dharma Sena started weeping.

While he was crying, Rudra got up, his face red, and placed his sword on the chest of Dharma Sena. 'You traitor, you tried to kill me with your poisoned soup. Your own deed killed your son. Arrest him!'

The Mauryan soldiers immediately arrested Dharma Sena. Rudra announced, 'All the wise men of the Massaga fort, please note one thing. You must surrender to the Mauryan ruler. Do not be fascinated by the wines and women of the barbarians. If you surrender and reveal all the truths, the Mauryan empire will take care of you. If you play with me like Dharma Sena, you are doomed. As a warrior, I seek to act rather than talk. This is the warning from the Mauryan commander. Don't take it lightly.'

A few elderly men came forward and said, 'Commander, we are with you. We lost our great ruler Ashvajit. Dharma Sena is his wife's brother. He fooled his sister and made way for Greeks. He is the real traitor. More than 5,000 men under the commander Rodrigus are hiding in the underground tunnels. They will come out once they receive signals from Dharma Sena. Be careful!'

'Do not worry. I will take care of it all. For a while, Dharma Sena was cheating me and I was about to take him at face value. Let me take charge of this fort,' replied Rudra.

Rudra decided to use Dharma Sena to trap the Greek satrap

and his soldiers. The Mauryan soldiers chained Dharma Sena.

It was late in the evening, and the bright moon was out in the sky. Rudra took Dharma Sena to the entrance of one of the underground tunnels.

Dharma Sena was yet to come out of the shock brought on by the death of his son. He could not understand what was going on. What would happen next?

7

Rudra ordered his soldiers to place a number of empty cages near the entrance to the underground tunnel.

He told Dharma Sena, 'Look, what I say now, you have to repeat loudly near the entrance of this tunnel. Not one single word more, not a single word less. You will say, "Commander Rodrigus, this is Dharma Sena here! The Mauryan commander believed the story I told him. I told him you have run away from this place with your men. He thought that there would be no resistance from the locals in the palace. He went down the hill with a promise to come back within three days to formalize the annexation of the Massaga fort. You and your men must be finding it difficult inside the tunnel. Since three more days are left for the arrival of Mauryans, please come out with your men and breathe the fresh air and enjoy good food. Leave your weapons in the tunnel as you will need to hide them again in three days. Come out one by one."'

As Dharma Sena shouted these words, the narrow entrance of the underground tunnel opened.

One by one, the soldiers began walking out, leaving their weapons inside. As each one came out, they were taken by the Mauryan soldiers into the cages placed nearby.

It took nearly three hours, but then all the soldiers were imprisoned in the cages. But one problem remained. Where was Rodrigus, the Greek satrap?

Dharma Sena was evading the process of identification.

Out of the many Greek soldiers, how could Rudra indentify Rodrigus? The council of ministers went home, and only Mauryan soldiers remained.

Rudra hit upon an idea. He released the caged Swastika and Visaka and brought them to where the Greeks had been stationed.

Swastika was asked to identify Rodrigus. She did so at once.

Rodrigus was tall, with well-shaped eyebrows. His long nose and cheekbones sat above an square jaw. His wrestler's shoulders were part of his burly physique. His forceful personality and base voice were a big part of his character. An air of arrogance surrounded him. 'Where did the arrogance come from? Is it a feeling of racial supremacy? What is it?' Rudra wondered.

'Rodrigus, you and your soldiers are prisoners of war. We will not harm you. But you should not try to hit back at us. You will have to carry out the jobs assigned by our Mauryan representatives.'

He asked his soldiers to disarm the Greeks, retrieve all the arms hidden in the underground tunnels and then jailed them.

By the time he was done, it was midnight. Now turning to Swastika, Rudra said, 'Now, Swastika, you are free. Your brother is free. You can do whatever you want.'

'Commander, you did what you promised,' Swastika said.

'Swastika, you saved my life. I still have an unfinished agenda. I am yet to complete my obligations to my beloved emperor, Chandragupta. I will always be grateful to you, Swastika.'

'Commander, the secret to happiness is freedom; the secret to freedom is courage. I will be courageously facing my life, as I did till now, Commander. You freed us. To the world you are one person, but to me you are the world.'

Swastika looked into the commander's eyes. 'Rudra, I love you. I have no one to support me. You saved me from the jaws of death. Will you take me as your life partner? Will you marry me? My heart has felt the love for you, which is invisible to the eye. Don't deny me your love, Commander.'

It was a question from her heart. Rudra was moved. He also owed gratitude to her since she had saved his life. Swastika continued, 'Commander, I suffered heavily in my childhood. Do not leave me in the hands of the barbarians. Dharma Sena, my uncle, is worse than the barbarians. We faced his cruelty for so long. Please, for heaven's sake, don't ignore my love. If you say no, suicide is the only option for me. Please Commander, take me as your life partner. You are my only ray of hope. You have revived my interest in life.'

Rudra could not control himself. Unmindful of the surroundings, he embraced her and said, 'Swastika, you have won my heart. I love you.' He kissed her on her forehead. 'Swastika, a kiss can beautify souls, hearts and thoughts. We are two angels with only one wing; we can only fly by embracing one another.'

Swastika could not escape from his tight embrace for a long time. She said, 'Commander, you gave me freedom at midnight, but you have imprisoned me with your tight embrace. I seem to have no escape from you.'

'Swastika, this ring of mine is the world's smallest handcuff. Yes, I gave you freedom at midnight. But my love has imprisoned you now. Marriage is a divine covenant and not a contract. I will marry you this night, this hour under the bright moonlight.' Saying this, he placed his ring on her finger.

'Commander, our marriage has been solemnized by your

golden ring. This ring starts our relationship, the beginning of which is a glance and the ending is eternity. I am happy to have been imprisoned by your heart, even though I got freedom from the barbarians at midnight. I receive my strength in loving you; I get strength from being loved by you, Commander.'

'Swastika, a flower cannot blossom without sunshine and a man cannot live without love. Now I can live with your love, Swastika. Take away the love and the earth will become a tomb, only when there is love, there is life—isn't it, Swastika?'

That was a long night for those two loving hearts which began to beat as one.

PART II

Sweetheart: Sour Thoughts

8

The next morning, Rudra took charge of the fort. He assembled the senior council of ministers.

'Gentlemen, as you are aware, this fort has come under the dominion of the Mauryan empire with immediate effect. Dharma Sena, Rodrigus and all the Greek soldiers are our prisoners. I will stay in this fort for the next two months. I will designate a representative of the Mauryan empire before leaving. We will not harm anyone. You are all citizens of our empire. Against those who abuse law and order, we will take tough action. Otherwise, the business will go on as usual. All of you will continue to serve in the same positions you occupy now.

'Meanwhile, Ashvajit's daughter and son will be released. They will stay in this palace for now. Their royal rights are restored.'

There was great applause, which conveyed the approbation of all the senior ministers. The news spread like fire among the citizens, who were happy with the outcome. They were happy to come into the empire of a Bharat ruler.

After his address to the council of ministers, Rudra went to the palace office and got busy with the day-to-day routine. He sent messages to Emperor Chandragupta who was camping in Taxila, the capital of Gandhara.

After a tiring day's work, he went to his accommodation. To his surprise, he was greeted by Swastika and Visaka, who had prepared a meal. He had good food and Visaka went to his room, while Swastika followed Rudra.

'Your Majesty, my queen, are you happy?' asked Rudra.

'I am not happy because I have come back to the palace, Commander. I am happy because I have found my man. As a whole forest becomes fragrant thanks to the existence of a single tree with sweet-smelling blossoms, so a family becomes famous thanks to the birth of a virtuous son. But my family regained its name with the arrival of a virtuous commander named Rudra.'

'Oh, my love, you are going overboard in praising me. We have now got into a wedlock which is more than an entanglement of hearts; it is rather the entwining of two lives. However you praise me, will henceforth come to you,' quipped Rudra.

'Commander, how did you conquer our impregnable fort?' Swastika asked.

'Yes, I will explain but on one condition: you must stop addressing me as "Commander", Swastika,' Rudra said.

'My karmic bond with you started with you as a commander. It is my own special pet name for you.' Swastika would not give up.

'If you feel that addressing me as Commander is romantic, I give you that privilege unhesitatingly Swastika.' Rudra gave in to her request.

'Let me come to the siege of the Massaga fort. I discovered that there were 5,000 Greek soldiers and 5,000 Asvaka soldiers along with more than 25,000 citizens staying inside. I also knew that enough provisions for a year were stored here.

'But I worked with my miners to tunnel beneath the fort walls to create an underground passage leading to the centre of this city. Your people stood terrified and unnerved when they saw me emerge with my army in the very centre of the city. But before I could imprison them, the Greek satrap went underground with 5,000 of his men. The rest is the history, as you know.'

'Commander, can we solemnize our marriage in the Shiva temple tomorrow morning? I want to announce to the world that I am your wife forever,' Swastika began pestering Rudra.

'Why are you in a hurry?' countered Rudra.'

'Maybe I am, but let me share my anxieties with you, Commander.'

9

Swastika began narrating the horrible woes she had faced since her childhood.

'Ashvajit, my father, was killed by Alexander's commanders when I was young. My mother Avantika was left with two young children—me and my brother. She did not know what to do, whether to surrender or to attack. She was going through utter confusion. She wanted to immolate herself as we follow the practice of sati.

'At that point her brother, Dharma Sena, used his cunning skills. He brainwashed her by using me and my infant brother. She was convinced to avert the futher killing of our tribe. Her individual sacrifice could save a community.'

'On the other hand, Dharma Sena spoke of your mother as a woman with no morality,' intervened Rudra.

'Commander, I do not expect anything better from him. He is the most cunning man our soil has ever produced. My mother thought she had to make the sacrifice so that she could save the tribe. Death cannot bring any benefit to the community, but her sacrifice could bring it—that was what she was forced to believe. What was that sacrifice? Her beauty was bartered to let the Asvakas come out of the clutches of death. She was enjoyed by the dirty commander for several nights on the advice and support of my uncle, Dharma Sena. She became the mistress of the Greek general.

'After being relieved of the threat of the attack, Dharma

Sena killed the Greek commander in charge and projected it as a killing by the rebels of the Asvaka tribe, who escaped from the fort after my father's death. My uncle was given the temporary role as a satrap till Rodrigus joined him three years later. Now he was the de facto ruler of the fort.

'Unable to bear the dirty game played by my uncle, my mother died, leaving us orphans. We were never allowed to pursue our education. We were only taught the Greek language so that we could be sold as slaves to a Greek commander later.

'My uncle did not want my brother to be physically fit as he could claim the throne as a legal heir of my father, the original ruler. Hence he incapacitated him by blinding him in a dirty game. My brother could have lost both his eyes, but fortunately, he lost only one.

'Not only that, but my uncle was forcing me to marry him so that I would not be a threat to him and his claim could be solidified. When I refused, he sold us to a Greek commander as slaves. We were waiting to be deported when you came.'

'Why did you agree to go to Greece, Swastika?' Rudra asked.

10

'It is better to be without a kingdom than to rule over a petty one; better to be without a friend than to befriend a rascal; better to be without a disciple than to have a stupid one; and better to be without a husband or family than to have a bad one. In the same way, I thought it would be better to go to Greece as a slave than agree to the forced marriage with my uncle,' Swastika said, with tears in her eyes.

'Swastika, do not cry. Everything will be all right. Happy days are here again. Don't worry, stop crying, I am with you,' Rudra consoled her.

'Commander, you might still believe that I was born of a mother with no moral values, whatever may be the reason for her behaviour,' Swastika said, looking deep into his eyes.

'Swastika, even from poison we extract nectar, we wash and take back gold if it has fallen in filth, receive the highest knowledge from a lowborn person; so also is a girl who possess virtuous qualities, even if she is born in a disreputable family. Now you are from a reputable family but you suffer from the stigma of the past. Now that I know about it, I accept you without any hesitation. Cry, forgive, and move on. Let your tears water the seeds of your happiness. No more worries, Swastika. A strong person gives forgiveness but a weak one gives permission. You are a strong-willed lady, forgive those who were cruel to you. I guarantee yours and your brother's life. It is my responsibility, Swastika,' Rudra thundered with all the sincerity in his being.

Hearing this, Swastika was very happy. 'Commander, the greatest achievement in my life thus far has been to love you and be loved by you. I need you because I love you. It is not the other way around. Ours is a mature love, Commander.' Rudra could see a glow in her eyes. She was saying this with all conviction.

Swastika continued. 'To love someone deeply gives you strength, and being loved by someone gives you courage. I have all the courage in the world now. It is a true happiness since I feel I am marrying my protective commander and a good friend.'

Rudra was moved. In order to lighten the emotionally charged atmosphere he added his humour. 'Swastika, marriage is a three-ring circle—engagement ring, wedding ring and suffering. Do you know that?'

Swastika retorted, 'But I can't wait to be married! Get ready, Commander.'

'Swastika, I am ready. Our love is expressed not just in our eyes but our minds as well. We are now soulmates—two halves of the same soul joining together to face life's journey,' Rudra replied, looking passionately into her eyes.

'Having faced difficulties since childhood, I am nervous about letting go of a good opportunity when it knocks at my door. I do not want to wait any longer. I am in a hurry. We should marry in the Shiva temple tomorrow, Commander.'

'The world's biggest power is the youth and beauty of women, Swastika. Now, when my Swastika says something, I have to follow, right?' Rudra remarked. Hearing this, Swastika opted for a tight embrace with her Commander, not even allowing a small space for the air to enter between them.

'Swastika, I understand your urgency, but I have not done anything in my life without informing my Guru Chanakya or my emperor. But this time, I will have to inform them of this important event only after its occurrence. Your urgency is making me breach my unshakable sincerity. Love is blind, and I have been impressed by your love.

'Let me fulfil your wish. Tomorrow morning, we will have our marriage solemnized in the Shiva temple of your fort, but on one condition. We have to marry once again in a grand function with my Guru, the emperor and my family present once we reach Pataliputra. Do you agree to this?'

'Whatever my Commander says,' said Swastika.

PART III

The Confession of a Greek Princess

11

Magha month, 305 BC.

While Rudra was camping in the Asvaka region, these sounds were reverberating against the sands of Taxila.

Samrat Chandragupt Ki Jaya Ho!
Raja Seleukos Ki Jaya Ho!
Bharat Aur Yavanas Ki Jaya Ho!
Commander Rudra Ki Jaya Ho!

The repeated chants of 'Rudra, Rudra!' were ringing bells in the mind of Helen, the Greek princess and daughter of the former general of Alexander and the present ruler of western India and Persia, Commander Seleukos.

Helen and Chandragupta were enjoying each other's company in the moonlight in the Taxila palace, facing the Jhelum river.

Chandragupta was a tall man, well-built and muscular and looked every inch a soldier, a Vrata Kshatriya. His dark-complexioned, shining face was cheerful, smiling and captivating, but a close observation revealed an inward seriousness. His chin indicated grim determination and an iron will. He wore a loincloth. It was tucked up at his waist and came halfway down to his ankles. He also wore a silk coat fastened in the front with tassels, a gold-laced upper cloth over his shoulders and a laced turban.

Helen was a tantalizing enigma, a stunningly beautiful

Greek woman. Her hands were white and she had a lovely face. She was irresistible for any man, the embodiment of feminine allure.

'Who is this Rudra, Samrat?' Helen asked Chandragupta.

'Why do you ask irrelevant questions at this pleasant time, when we are enjoying each others' company? He is the commander-in chief of our army,' quipped Chandragupta.

'As the public were praising him, I wondered who he was. Anyway, let us leave it for now, Samrat. Do you know what? Once you went riding with a body of soldiers on the banks of this river. I saw you as a tall and powerful warrior on a horse. I was smitten by your demeanour and air of majesty royalty. I learned you were Samrat Chandragupta, the brave emperor of the Mauryan empire, but I knew my father would never permit me to marry a Hindu warrior.'

'But, Helen, I too fell in love with you when I saw you, a woman of startling beauty amongst the bevy of handmaidens. I learned that you were the daughter of Seleukos, but I did not care who your father was. I wanted to spend the rest of my life in your company—come what may. That is why we exchanged letters through pigeons.

'I confessed my burning desire to my learned counsel, Chanakya. I was confused about whether my desire was right, since I was already married to Queen Durdhara. Chanakya told me that the only way to seek your hand was to declare war against Seleukos. I won you through the war with your father, Helen.

'Do you love me, Helen? Will you not miss your Greek family? I do not want you to feel sundered from them.'

12

'Samrat, are you asking me whether I might want to go back to Greece?

'Samrat, I have become a native of this land. This land of eternal mystery has caught and tamed me. I love a peepal leaf now more than a Greek vase, a mango more than a fig, mustard oil more than olive, the cow more than the horse, the peacock more than the hen, the kokil more than the nightingale, the Himalayas more than Olympus, Pataliputra more than my native town, and above all, Samrat Maurya more than any Greek warrior,' said Helen.

'Samrat, love is composed of a single soul inhabiting two bodies. We may give without loving, but we cannot love without giving. I am giving up Greece for Bharat.'

'Helen, love is like a war—easy to begin but very hard to stop. We have already begun love, and now we cannot stop.' Chandragupta agreed with her.

'Samrat, I have been living in this region for more than ten years. I have learnt your dances and classical music, I have learnt Sanskrit and Prakrit. I think I was born on this soil in my last birth. No wonder I am perfectly at ease here. Even my parents could not understand why I was so fascinated by your land and your company.'

'Helen, tell me about your father, Seleukos. Why was he so keen on conquering our kingdom?'

'Samrat, my father was one of the trusted generals of

Alexander. He accompanied Alexander during his invasion of your land. When asked by his companions about whom he was leaving his kingdom, Alexander had replied with his dying breath, "To the strongest. I foresee a great contest over my body." While his generals were fighting with one another in order to see who was the strongest, after the wives, sons, half-brother and mother of the great conqueror had been murdered, Samrat, you conquered the land east of the Indus, with the exception of a small bit in dakshin Bharat. However, my father was feeling secure on his throne at Babylon. He had come out very well from the general scramble. The far-flung empire of Alexander was split into three parts—the Greek, the Egyptian and the Asian. The first two went to two other generals, the third fell in the hands of my father.

'How and why did he come into your kingdom? I will tell you now.

'My father had become the master of all the provinces of the old empire of Alexander from the borders of Syria eastwards up to the Indus, including Bactria, Sogdiana, Aria, Arachosia, Parapamasadai, Gedrosia and the whole of Persia and Babylonia, and had crowned himself the king. He resolved to take this opportunity of recovering the land west of the Hyphasis and the Indus valley, which had been annexed by you.

'My father had heard vague accounts of the size of your empire and army. He had also heard much about the splendour of the city of Pataliputra, and of Taxila and Ujjain, which were said to surpass Susa and Babylon in magnificence.

'He felt sure that he could easily defeat you, the young man whom he had seen at Boukephala as a suppliant for Alexander's help. He considered Poros Senior to be a far more formidable opponent, and yet he and Alexander had defeated Poros and made him a vassal. And now, Poros had been murdered in mysterious circumstances, my father, proud of his great personal strength and courage, took you very lightly before waging a war against you. Senior Poros had been killed, Ambhi of Taxila committed suicide under mysterious circumstances, and my father thought the best thing would be to get his satraps into the Indus region and conquer you and make you a vassal.

'But how did you win over my father, Samrat?'

13

'Helen, listen to this tale,' began Chandragupta.

'Your father sent an ultimatum to me from Bactria, asking me, on the threat of an armed invasion and conquest, to surrender the Indus valley and territories to the east of the Indus and to recognize him as my emperor, and pay a tribute of ten million gold *suvarnas* per year. I consulted Chanakya, and sent the following reply:

"His Majesty Emperor Chandragupta, the Beloved of the Gods, sends his greetings to King Seleukos of Babylon, and categorically refuses every one of his ridiculous demands. There is no more justification for his demanding the cession of territory or tribute from Emperor Chandragupta than for Emperor Chandragupta to demand cession of territory or tribute from him. Emperor Chandragupta requests him not to be rash enough to press these absurd demands and invade his lands once again. He would be forced to imitate, on a larger and more disastrous scale, the celebrated flight of his master Alexander, who left the bodies of three-fourths of his troops in this land for the jackals and vultures to feed on. If, however, he persists in this foolish course and invades the kingdoms, Mauryan troops will be ready to deal with the living invaders."

'Samrat, yes, my father was upset on seeing your reply. He, who had crossed the Hydaspes with Alexander and defeated the great Poros, was being insulted like this by this boy supplicant of yesterday! He resolved to teach you a lesson that you would never forget. He decided to advance on Pataliputra itself, and capture it. He gathered an army of 1,00,000 Greeks and 2,00,000 Sogdians, Bactrians, Persians, Scythians, Sakas and others anxious for the spoils of the Indus region. Then he marched from Bactria into Parapamasadai at the head of this enormous and well-equipped force.'

'Helen, meanwhile I discussed the plan of the campaign with Chanakya. He said, "We are so strong that we had better induce the enemy to cross the Indus, and then smash his forces." This time it would be a real battle, and not a battle of intrigue. This is what happened.

'I agreed with him in abandoning Pushkalavati, and in leaving the Indus crossing undefended, and concentrating 4,00,000 infantry, 20,000 cavalry, 4,000 chariots and 6,000 elephants at Taxila as he suggested. But Chanakya also pointed out that the generals of Alexander had adopted the methods of our kings, and were relying on intrigue to a large extent. Seleukos considered himself to be a master of intrigue. We had received a note from our spies, warning us that Seleukos had approached Abhisara, Arsakes, Pushkaradatta, the son of Pushakara, and Malayaketu for their aid against us. They, being men of honour, at once communicated this to our spy who had, on my instructions, allowed those princes to pretend to fall in with Seleukos's offer. So, we would trap some of the Greeks like cattle. Indeed, Chanakya doubted there would be a battle at all. But I hoped I would have something to do.'

'Then how did the war unfold, Samrat?'

14

'When your father advanced into our territory with his mighty army, he was surprised at the place being undefended, and assumed that we were terrified of him. Then he marched further, crossing the Indus. He was greeted by the army of Malayaketu and Pushakara, the kings of Punjab and Kashmir, who pretended to accept his authority.

'He must have thought his victory was made so simple. The disguised loyalists persuaded him to attack our territories of Taxila from the back. Seleukos followed their suggestion.

'While his army was marching towards the back of Taxila, he was surrounded on all sides by our Mauryan forces. Then, to his dismay, even the proclaimed loyalists such as Malayaketu attacked his army from within. "Traitors!" shouted Seleukos.

'His army was massacred by mine. He understood that there was no point in fighting further. He decided to sign the Treaty of Taxila.

'The rest is history for you, Helen. The treaty had the following clauses:

Your father ceded considerable territory to me—Herat, Kandahar and the Kabul valley came into my kingdom.

I gave him 500 trained war elephants to play a key role in his future battles.

And lastly, the best of all gifts—you were offered to me.'

'Samrat, did you conquer me or my father?'

'Perhaps both, my dear darling,' replied Chandragupta.

'Your father must have thought that the marriage between us would cement the alliance and friendship between Greece and my kingdom. That sealed the treaty between us.

'Now, Helen—you answered the first part—how your father gave you to me. But you have to answer me the next part—why was he so keen to conquer my kingdom?'

'Samrat, I am coming to that question. I have to start with Alexander the Great, so that you can understand the picture clearly.

'But before starting the story, I need to receive a tight hug from my Samrat.' She kissed him passionately before proceeding.

15

'Samrat let me begin with Alexander the Great, as promised yesterday. His was a striking personality. Even before the consummation of her marriage, his mother Olympias dreamt that a thunderbolt fell upon her womb and kindled a fire that spread all around and was then extinguished. She firmly believed that Alexander, her son, would burst into different parts of the world like the thunderbolt and the flames. He could be extinguished only after he became the lord of the world and would not succumb to any other enemy but a natural death. She sowed the seeds of his vision to go and conquer the very ends of the earth. Alexander's territorial ambition began there.

'While Olympias had a dream of a thunderbolt in her womb, Alexander's father Philip dreamt that he had put upon his wife's womb a seal which had a lion as a device. In terror he peeped into the room where his wife was sleeping. He was surprised to see a huge serpent sleeping with her on her bed.

'When he consulted the fortune-tellers they told him that the serpent was the god Ammon and that a son as brave as a lion would be born to Olympias and Ammon, and Philip would lose one of his eyes for peeping when the god and Olympias were together. Philip did lose one of his eyes, but of course, a son as brave as a lion, Alexander, was born. Even as a boy, the royal element was visible in his personality.

'An interesting thing happened when Alexander was thirteen years old. A horse-dealer offered a horse to Alexander's father, King Philip, for 130 talents, which was a huge amount of gold. Because no one could tame the animal, Philip was not interested.

'The dealer did not know where the horse came from. One day he had seen it wandering around his area. No one knew the truth about the horse. It was called Bucephalus (because its head was like an ox's). The horse was a massive creature with a massive head, a strong and beautiful body, black in colour. It had a peculiarly shaped white mark on its forehead. The dealer told Philip that the destined king of the world would be the one who rode Bucephalus.

'Philip could not see the point of paying such a high price for an unruly horse and ordered it to be taken away. According to legend, Alexander called out that it was a shame to waste such an animal because of poor riders.

'Philip turned to look at his son. "Alexander, what do you mean?"'

'"I can ride this horse," Alexander replied. "It just needs the right rider."

'Philip scoffed. "My attendants have been working with horses most of their lives, but you know better?" Alexander nodded, his mouth setting into stubborn lines.

'"I know it would be shameful to throw away a good horse because people haven't been paying attention to the kind of animal he is." Alexander had realized that the stallion was nervous, unsure of his handlers, trusting no one but himself. He was also an animal filled with pride and a sense of self-awareness unusual for his kind. Pausing for a moment, Alexander said with confidence, "I know this horse and I'll make a wager for the price of the horse that I can ride him."'

'Philip reluctantly agreed, thinking that Alexander would

be humbled and think more carefully about future bets. At the same time, he admired the fire in the boy and didn't want to quench it. He watched as Alexander slowly approached Bucephalus and carefully took the bridle below the chin. Alexander knew a frightened horse would jerk his head and he wanted to be certain the animal could feel his own confidence. He gently stroked the centre of Bucephalus' nose and lips with his finger, remembering a horse can whisk a fly off its ears. Alexander calmly moved towards the animal, placing his other hand on the horse's body, rubbing and scratching the flank, moving forward with his hand to slowly massage the neck.

'Alexander knew horses notice hand and head motions and respond quickly; he knew that because horses were not verbal animals, words were unnecessary to elicit a response. Alexander knew that horses, as animals who were preyed upon, often feared shadows, so he led Bucephalus by the reins, touching him gently, whispering comforting words, letting the horse see the movement of sun and shadow, learning there was nothing to fear in this strange field though he was surrounded by strangers.

'Slowly, Alexander eased onto the horse's back. The animal stood alert but calm, turning his ears back in an attempt to understand this confident boy on his back. Alexander worked the reins and leg pressure just enough to take his horse from a trot to a canter as everyone held their breath. He gave the horse more rein, allowing Bucephalus to move into a gallop. Keeping the horse's head up, he urged him into a full run. After working the horse for a while in view of an ever-growing audience, Alexander stopped Bucephalus in front of Philip. A cheering crowd surrounded father, horse and son. With tears of laughter and joy, pride showing in his gestures, Philip said

"Alexander my son, Macedon is too small. You need to find another kingdom worthy of you!" And thus began the legend.

'Alexander rode Bucephalus in many battles. The warhorse contested the difficulties of the muddy riverbanks, biting and kicking all his foes. There was something about this horse that struck a responsive chord in even the most jaded viewer.

'When he was equipped with royal trappings, he would suffer no one but Alexander to mount him, although at other times he would allow anyone to do so. It is said that even when the horse was wounded in an attack, he would not allow Alexander to mount any other steed. When Bucephalus died, Alexander performed the funeral ceremonies, and built around his tomb a city that he named after him.'

16

'Samrat, if his birth and childhood is throwing up surprises, his upbringing by his teachers during his adolescence will be still more interesting.

'Alexander's father was very fond of women, but Alexander himself was not. One day, just before he retired to bed, Philip made a beautiful dancing girl lie on Alexander's bed in order to tempt him. But when Alexander saw the woman, he turned back in disgust and slept with his friend in the next room.

'His mother appointed his teacher Leonidas to counteract his father's weaknesses. Leonidas taught him to live abstemiously. Alexander often recalled his teacher's maxim: "The best appetizer for breakfast is a night's march. The best appetizer for dinner is a light breakfast." The less one's refreshments, the greater his independence and capacity for achievements.

'While his mother appointed Leonidas, his father appointed Aristotle, the wisest man in Greece as his tutor for three years to enable Alexander to gain wisdom. Alexander would tell everyone, "My father gave me life but Aristotle taught me how to live."'

'Which qualities did he inherit from each parent, Helen?'

'Samrat, from his father Alexander inherited his courage and an immense capacity for work. From his mother he inherited a vivid imagination, great willpower and a mysterious affinity with the occult.'

'Occult? Why does a military man require this?' Samrat asked in surprise.

'Samrat, you are surprised? Alexander's beliefs brought him to this ancient land. His mother kept a constant watch on his progress. She was the backbone behind all his ambition. She would ask him about his interactions with the philosopher Aristotle. One day, towards the end of his three years with Aristotle, Olympias wanted to find out from her son about his learning.

'Olympias said to Alexander, "Son, you are now sixteen. Now that you've finished your studies, what do you want to do next? You were born to achieve, and you should not limit yourself to your father's kingdom."'

'"Mother, I am going to conquer the world," replied Alexander.

'"Do you know where the world ends, my son?" asked Olympias.

'"The world ends with the ocean visible from the Hindu Kush mountains. The conquest of the Indus basin will complete the conquest of the world, Mother. My first target is Persia, then the Indus basin. Aristotle told me about these boundaries," said Alexander.

'"Excellent, my son. You were born to conquer the world. Go to the very ends of the earth, to the shores of the great sea past the Indian Gulf and the soil of the Persian Gulf, Egypt and Macedonia. Make the boundaries of the earth the boundaries of your dominion. My son, unite the world under you, and abolish all artificial distinctions of race and kingdom. But my son, do not forget the elixir of life and the mother of all missiles that can be found in the land beyond the Hindu Kush. Your conquest will be complete only with all this—the world, the elixir of life and mother of all missiles. Have you asked Aristotle about this?"

"'Mother, I came to know of ambrosia, the elixir of life. It is the drink of our Greek gods and confers immortality. Aristotle told me about this while teaching Homer's poems to me. The consumption of ambrosia was typically reserved for divine beings, I was told.'

"'Only one human was ever permitted to consume ambrosia: Tantalus. But Tantalus planned to steal it and give it to other mortals. He was cursed and so are all the humans who are denied ambrosia.'

"'But Aristotle told me that the word ambrosia is linked to the Sanskrit word amrit, and the drops of the elixir of life fell on the ancient land of Bharat.'"

"'My son, you must conquer the land of Bharat as well as the amrit it holds.'"

'Helen, did the Greeks know of our Puranas and our myths?'

'Samrat, you will be surprised to know that the Greeks have long spoken of Bharat, your land, as the sacred territory of Dionysus and Heracles. Dionysus refers to your god Shiva and Heracles as your "Hare Krishna". Our historians clearly mention chronicles of the Puranas as sources of the myth of Dionysus and Heracles. Where did you think I received my inspiration to fall in love with your land, Samrat? It comes from these connections between my land and yours.'

17

Helen's story continued as followed:

'Son, Alexander, Have you been taught about Heracles?'

'Yes, Mother, Aristotle taught me about Heracles. Not only that, but Aristotle also told me about the similarities between Heracles and Hare Krishna of the Hindu land,' Alexander replied. 'He spoke of many similarities between them. 'Both were born to a mortal mother and a divine father. When Heracles was born, the goddess Hera, wife of Zeus, sent two serpents to kill him. This is similar to how Kamsa, Krishna's uncle, sought to kill him shortly after his birth.

'Mother, I am keen to conquer the land of Lord Krishna. I have heard of mythological weapons that can be found there.'

'Son, what did you say? Where did you hear about these weapons?'

'Mother, I was listening to the stories told by the learned Aristotle. He spoke of the divine twins, Apollo and Artemis.

'Homer wrote, "Apollo's arrows killed the fearsome python, piercing it with his darts." Apollo's arrows are so powerful. Not only that, but his sister Artemis, the goddess of the hunt, is so powerful that she is always depicted with a bow and arrow.

'Aristotle told me that some of the arrows from the land of Krishna are even more powerful. Since I heard about this, my mind has been keen to recover these weapons, Mother. There is a reference to a particular kind of mantra-based weapon that was used along with bows and arrows and is called a "Brahmastra". This weapon could release great energy with pinpoint accuracy. It brings about complete and utter destruction. The creator, Brahma, had also created a weapon even more powerful than the Brahmastra, called the Brahmashira. The Brahmashira was never used in war, as it was four times more powerful than the Brahmastra. Only the heroes, Arjuna and Ashwathama, possessed the knowledge to summon the weapon. The weapon was also believed to cause severe environmental damage. The land where the weapon was used became barren and all life in and around that area ceased to exist, as both women and men became infertile.'

'Alexander, my son, you are the offspring of a god, you were born to achieve resounding triumphs. Hence, you must march on my son, and begin your conquest. Emerge as the lord of Persia and Asia and go to the very ends of the earth, conquer the land of Lord Krishna along with the mythical treasures. Good luck, my son.'

Chandragupta said, 'Oh, Alexander came here for so many reasons! I am surprised indeed that he knew about our gods.'

'Samrat, don't be surprised. To confirm your belief, let me share another fact with you. The historians who travelled with Alexander mentioned that Porus's soldiers carried an image of Heracles. He was referring to the statue of Krishna your soldiers carried. For me, Heracles is a form of Krishna or vice versa.'

'Very interesting, Helen. Now tell me, how did Alexander start his conquest?'

'Samrat, I need to remind you that we are newly wedded. I need your love now more than Alexander's story of conquest. Let us speak of that tomorrow. I do not want to waste this night when my Samrat is next to me. You are a great warrior, so come, start the war of unstoppable love tonight.' Helen fondly kissed her Samrat, inviting him into her tight embrace.

18

The next day, Samrat Chandragupta persuaded Helen to continue the story of Alexander and his conquest.

'Samrat, now you will hear from me the great journey of Alexander from a boy king just crowned to the conqueror of the world and an enemy at your doorstep,' Helen said.

'When Alexander became king, there were many other claimants to the throne. He unleashed a reign of terror on his opponents. Many were killed and the survivors fled. When Thebes started to show signs of not bending to Alexander, he came with a large army and crushed the city. Except for the house of the great poet Pindar, all houses were razed to the ground and the inhabitants were either sold as slaves or killed.

'With his kingdom under control, Alexander came back to Macedonia and started to plan his great expedition to Persia and Asia. His massive army of 35,000 men crushed the Persian army and took Sardius, the Persian stronghold.

'From there he moved into Phyrgia. The citizens took him to the temple and showed him the chariot of Gordius. The yoke was tied by a great knot and the citizens told him that if he undid the knot and freed the yoke, they would proclaim him king. Alexander pulled out his sword and in a single stroke cut the knot and freed the yoke. The citizens were horrified. The priest told Alexander that since he had taken a shorter route and cheated, he would become emperor in the same way: he would be cheated and his life would be cut short.

The battle-hardened Alexander dismissed this prophecy. He was on the quest for immortality anyway.

'After Phyrgia, the next confrontation was with the great King Darius. His army was routed and Darius fled, leaving his family behind. After this, Damascus fell and Tyre, the Syrian fort, was brought to its knees by a siege that lasted seven months. Alexander had the giddy confidence of victory and his reputation was so great that Egypt, Jerusalem and the holy land were captured without a fight. The local people welcomed him. Alexander founded Alexandria, a port city named after himself, to rival Tyre.

'Come spring and Darius challenged Alexander with chariots, elephants and a vast army. Though outnumbered, the Greeks still won a famous victory and Darius fled again. Arbela, Babylon, Susa and finally Persepolis fell to Alexander. Darius was murdered by one of his own generals.

'At last, Alexander had completed his planned expedition. He had captured Persia, but the East had captured Alexander. The lure of ambrosia made him continue east.

'He charted a straight path to Bharat and the Indus by passing through Bactria. Alexander knew that he could not hold his empire by force alone. The conquered kings and satraps offered their daughters in marriage to him to cement their ties. But the Bactrian princess was an exception. She was truly beautiful and Alexander took her as his bride willingly.

'Southeast of Bactria and Persia, Alexander began his march towards the land of gold and diamonds. The land of ambrosia and the Brahmastra. He crossed the Khyber Pass and marched till he reached the banks of Hydaspes, and the river kingdom of Taxila, the very Taxila that you conquered, Samrat.'

19

Helen's narrative continued as follows:

'On his way to Taxila, Alexander the Great camped at a place. He encountered a strange man. This man, dressed in a loincloth, would meditate for hours in a secluded spot near Alexander's camp. For several days, Alexander saw this sage seated in a lotus position and meditating, looking towards the horizon. To Alexander, this sage seemed like a lazy man, a recluse who had dropped out of life's race. One day, the great warrior, unable to contain his curiosity, approached the sage and asked, "Don't you have anything to do besides sitting and dreaming?"

'The sage sat there unmoved. Alexander continued, "I see you every morning, evening and afternoon in the same place. You have not moved an inch. You must be a lazy fellow!"

'The sage did not speak a word. Irritated by his silence, Alexander probed, "Tell me what your goal in life is."

'Now the sage smiled a little and said, "Great warrior, you must first tell me about your goal in life before I tell you mine." Outraged, Alexander thundered, "Don't you know I am Alexander? I am out to conquer the world."'

'"What do you want to do after you have conquered the world?" the sage asked.'

'"I will then possess all the gold and all the elephants and horses in the world," said Alexander, his lip curling in disdain.'

"And then?"

"Then I will have all men as my slaves."

"And then?"

"Then I will sit on my throne, relax and enjoy myself."

'The sage smiled. "That is precisely what I am doing right now. Why are you bothering me? Please leave me alone and go ahead with your conquests."

'Alexander sought fulfilment in the conquest of the outer world, while the sage searched for peace in the inner domain. "My consciousness experiences the world as a battlefield whereas the sage's consciousness experiences the same world as the field of self-realization. How much more do I need to be happy? While the sage ponders, how can I be happy?"

"'I don't understand the mentality of the sages of the Asian land. I think I am going to experience the mysterious philosophies of these Indian sages," Alexander said to Sasi Gupta, his newly appointed interpreter.

'Sasi Gupta told Alexander, "Our kings are monarchs, but they cannot change the caste or customs of their people without the blessing of these Brahmins and sages. They wield tremendous influence over the kings and the people."

"'I like philosophers but they must keep to their sphere and not meddle in politics, otherwise they will be killed in my regime," Alexander said angrily.

'The next day, Alexander's troops moved and Alexander was galloping on his horse. Suddenly, an old man with an angry face and uncombed hair and a host of sores and ulcers stopped Alexander's horse.

'Alexander wondered who the strange man was. Was he a philosopher too?

'The man began speaking. "You must be the one I have been waiting for, for 2,500 years. Your horse has a bindi, the dot on the forehead. It is the same bindi that Draupadi, Panchali, the wife of Pandavas wore."

"'You do not know about your own horse. This horse, Ashva, was one which conquered many kingdoms and was used to perform the Ashwamedh Yagna of Emperor Dharma, the eldest of the Pandavas. This yagna was performed after the Kurukshetra war which killed many of Dharma's cousins and their warriors. A horse would be let loose and would be allowed to roam free for a year. Kingdoms that allowed the horse to pass would automatically agree to accept Emperor Dharma's suzerainty. These kingdoms did not have to battle the emperor. After a year, the Ashamedh yagna had to be performed. After the yagna, the horse had to be sacrificed and buried the next day. But the previous night, the horse which had conquered many kingdoms was fit to be treated like an emperor. The queen had to sleep with the horse."

'Draupadi refused to perform that ritual. She told Dharma, "Emperor, I was made to marry five husbands due to a mistake. Now you want me to sleep with a horse for a night. Even though it may be a symbolic act, pardon me, I can't do it. But to respect the rituals, I am placing my white bindi on the forehead of the horse. Please treat this as the completion of the rituals."

"'Dharma agreed to her request and her white bindi was placed on the horse's forehead. The horse was sacrificed and buried the next day at Kurukshetra."

"'Kshatriya warrior, your horse has the same white bindi on his forehead and looks like Ashva, the sacrificed horse. When Ashva permits someone to ride him, that person must be the greatest warrior of this Kali Yuga. Your horse has brought you to Bharat. It will win kingdoms for you. Its memories from its previous birth will take you to Kurukshetra and you will receive several secrets unlocked by your horse."

"'I was known as Ashwathama in the last yuga, named Suryakanta in this Kali Yuga due to the curse of that cunning Krishna during war. I can help you uncover several secrets which you are searching for. After all, I was one of the two warriors who knew how to use the 'Brahmastra'." Ashwathama finished his long story.

"'What? You know about the weapon? You are not able to even stand. You claim to come from the era of Heracles? Don't blabber to me, get away from here. I have no time for these rumour-mongers like you who wander like ghosts." Alexander was furious.

'Ignoring the old man, Alexander marched on with his warriors towards Taxila. Ashwathama looked at them and remarked, "You will need my assistance, and you will come back to me soon. You may ignore me now, but it cannot be for too long...."'

Helen went on, 'Alexander learnt that the old king of Taxila had died and that Omphis (Ambhi) had succeeded him. Ambhi sent an emissary formally offering his submission.

'Alexander thought the Indian princes were more sensible than the tribal heads, who did not submit to him so easily. He asked Sasi Gupta, "In an unknown land, I can never be sure. Who wants to join whom? Is Omphis reliable?"

'Sasi Gupta was spontaneous in his response. "The kings of the nearby kingdoms, Porus and Abhisara, want to team up with Ambhi to fight us. But Ambhi does not trust Porus. He is insecure; he wants to finish Porus with our support. But the Brahmins in Taxila are against us. They are trying to oppose us. Hence Ambhi is pretending to listen to them."

'"Again, the Brahmins seem to be troubled with my arrival," Alexander remarked.

'Just before the gates of Taxila, Alexander was received by none other than its King Omphis reconfirming his allegiance to the great conqueror.

'When Alexander rode into the vast meadow at the entrance of the city, he was puzzled when he saw the number of Brahmins stamping upon the ground. He asked them through his interpreter why they were behaving like that.

'The leader of the Brahmins said, "Oh, Alexander, each man can possess only as much of earth as we have trodden upon. You, on the other hand, think you own the earth and continuously disturb the peace of the world. Do not forget that when you die, you will possess just so much of the earth as will suffice to make a grave for your bones. That is what we mean to signify by our stamping on the ground."

'Alexander shouted back at them, "Just because we die one day, why should we be content to occupy only six feet of earth? Where then is the spirit of adventure, the unique glory of man, if we do not roam the lands and seas? Tell me where you live and who your teachers are and what you do all day long."

'The Brahmins replied, "We pass time in a wood a few miles from here. Our gurus are Dandiswami (Dandis) and Kalyana Swamy (Kalinos). We eat fruits and herbs and drink only water. We wander about in the wood during the day, meditating on God and discussing the problems of life and death. We sleep in the almshouses. Sometimes we spend our nights on pallets made of leaves."

'When Alexander sent his soldier to bring Dandiswami to his camp, the sage refused outright. However, he commended Alexander for his desire to acquire philosophical wisdom in spite of his being an emperor.

'Then Alexander met Kalyana Swamy (Kalinos), who was very receptive to him. Kalinos ate and drank with appetite and delighted one and all with his conversation. Alexander accepted him warmly. "From now on, you are my friend. I cannot allow you to go back. Grace the court as my honoured guest. Combine the wisdom of your race and ours and both of us shall profit."

"Very well," said Kalinos.

'Alexander asked Kalinos why Dandiswami refused to see him. He told Kalinos, "A religion which can produce men of such indomitable spirit must have merit in it. It must enforce a spiritual discipline as rigid as that in our Macedonians."

'Kalinos was surprised. "Sir, you are very interested in religious matters as well as issues relating to war."

"Kalinos, I am fascinated by the mysterious and the unknown and I have an overpowering desire to delve deeper and deeper into it," said Alexander. "You are a Dandiswami in action, sir," exclaimed Kalinos.

'At that time, the old man claiming to be Ashwathama came in and asked Alexander, "Have you thought of my proposal to assist you in getting what you really search for? You can ask Kalyana Swamy if you want to know more about me." Saying this, he vanished into the woods.'

21

'Alexander asked Kalinos, "Who is this old man who claims to know all about Brahmastra? Is he a mad man? He also says he will also unravel the amrit. Can I take him seriously?"

"'Sir, I have to explain to you about the Chiranjivis, who are immortals. You won't believe it, but Ashwathama is one of the immortals. These immortals are links between the various yugas in our stories. They carry secrets from one yuga to another."

"'Kalinos, it is interesting, I can unlock the secrets of Brahmastra and amrit which are buried in this ancient land. Tell me more about the Chiranjivis. Why does Ashwathama behave like a mad man even though he is a Chiranjivi?"

"'The shloka goes, 'Ashwathama Balir Vyaso Hanuman-shcha Vibhishanaha Krupaha Parashuramasaha Saptaitey Chiranjivaha.' Its meaning is, 'Ashwathama, King Mahabali, Vyasa, Hanuman, Vibhishana, Kripacharya and Parashuram are the seven death-defying or imperishable personalities.' Ashwathama comes first in the shloka of the Chiranjivis, as he is a partial incarnation of Lord Shiva. This makes him the twelfth Rudra."

"'Where do they live, Kalinos? If I meet them I can unlock the secrets of amrit and Brahmastra. Do they live here?"

"'No sir, they live under an assumed identity. Unless one is blessed, he cannot see or interact with them. Only Ashwathama being a negative Chiranjivi, is wandering the land," Kalinos clarified.

"'All the Chiranjivis, including Ashwathama, will assemble at the time of the birth of Kalki at the end of this Kali Yuga, after 4,32,000 years. We have just completed 2,500 years of the Kali Yuga. It is stated that Kalki will be a man from all religions, and will be born in the Dravida Desham near Thamira Bharani river in a village called Sambala Gramam. Kalki will ride a white horse with a bindi on its forehead, like your horse."

"'Interesting, Kalinos, can you brief me on each of these Chiranjivis?"'

"'There are seven immortals: Ashwathama, Bali, Vyasa, Hanuman, Vibhishan, Kripacharya and Parashuram. They symbolize certain higher ideals. The people here wear 'rakshas' with seven knots. Each knot indicates one of the Chiranjivis. This is a symbolic prayer for long life like that of the Chiranjivis. King Bali was immortalized because even Vishnu had to humble himself as Vamana to conquer him. He stands out for his valour and charity—two great qualities. Bali knew fully well who Vamana was. Yet, he prepared to surrender all he had to his Lord. So this man of grace is still revered. It is said that he is living in *patal lok*, beneath the earth."

"'Vyasa was the great scholar and writer, who wrote the Mahabharata, as it happened, and was also the author of the *Srimad Bhagavatam*. Vyasa is another immortal, a shining beacon of erudition and wisdom. He represents the continuity of erudition and scholarship."

"'Hanuman exemplifies selflessness, courage, devotion, energy, strength and righteous conduct. He stands for the potential that is inherent in all of us. He also represents the air, the atmosphere and thus the life-breath—the *prana*. Mother Sita is believed to have bestowed on him the boon which made Hanuman ever youthful, energetic and immortal."

"'Vibhishan had unshakable faith in what he believed. He was a fearless counsellor of righteousness even when all around him were given to sycophancy. As a follower of right conduct, Vibhishan survived unscathed while tragedy befell his brother Ravana, the unrighteous king and his followers."

"'Kripacharya was an extraordinary teacher. To him, all pupils were equal. A guru like Dronacharya favoured Arjuna and sacrificed an equally if not more promising student—he asked Ekalavya for his right thumb. Kripacharya, on the other hand, upheld the highest standards expected of a teacher. He was impartial."

"'Parashuram was a master of martial arts. No one could beat him—whether the tools were *astras*, *shastras* or divine weapons. He had no temporal ambition. Had he wished, he would have been the greatest Chakravarti Samrat the land had ever known. But he lived a hermit's life. He was also one who never hesitated to admit a mistake. Parashuram symbolizes excellence and strength, tempered by humility. He will reappear as the martial instructor of the forthcoming last avatar of Vishnu—Kalki."

"'These seven immortals exemplify certain basic truths, laws and standards of ethical behaviour which transcend time, locale and generation. They are universal and immutable. Their immortality is, therefore, not mere deathlessness—it is the immortalizing of each divine principle they stand for and uphold even in the face of adversity and pressure."

"'Now coming to Ashwathama. He is a negative Chiranjivi cursed to live till the end of Kali Yuga. He is keen to die but he cannot. He has to struggle for the whole Kali Yuga."

"'Kalinos, why do you call Ashwathama a cursed Chiranjivi?"

"'Aswathama, the son of Guru Dronacharya, was a mighty warrior. He had even learnt the art of invoking the Brahmastra, the ultimate weapon of destruction. The Brahmastra is unique in that it can be used to target anything with pinpoint accuracy and can seek and destroy. Also, the destructive power could be controlled. It is flexible enough to cause a bird to be killed. If an archer invokes Brahmastra, it not only destroys the target but also leads to a famine for twelve years in the region where it is employed. If it is invoked twice, then it can even lead to draining of the entire ocean. In the war between the Pandavas and Kauravas, Ashwathama was on the side of the Kauravas.'"

"'One day, after the war was over and when the Pandavas were gone, he and a posse of men entered their camp by stealth and killed all the male members in complete disregard of the prevailing ethics of warfare. He invoked the Bramastra against the Pandavas. He was later overpowered and arrested by the Pandavas. His life was spared but his crown jewel—a gem—was prised out of his head. He was condemned to forget his *astra* skills, live forever, his wounds festering, never healing. It was a warning to future generations that a great warrior's life, bereft of good conduct, is a life given to eternal suffering. That is karmic retribution. Ashwathama's flawed immortality is a grim reminder of the consequences of unethical behaviour.'"

"'Oh! I see. This is why the old man is wandering and I could not see any traces of the warrior in him.'"

"'Ashwathama may have forgotten the rules for initiating the Brahmastra, but he can give us the clues to find it. We can summon his memory. We have to use him for this purpose,' Kalinos added.

"'Right Kalinos. Let me go back to my camp. Tomorrow I will be visiting the Taxila university campus. You must accompany me during my stay here and later. I cannot trust the crooks here. They mislead me.'

"'I am always at your disposal, my king.'"

22

'Alexander gave his army a complete rest at Taxila and boosted their morale with equestrian and gymnastic contests. He began his preparations for the war with Porus, the king who had not accepted the supremacy of Alexander, unlike the other kings.

'While the preparations went on, Alexander visited the University of Taxila with Omphis. They took a round of various departments. The Ayurveda department, veterinary science, medicine, surgery, metallurgy, literature, the study of the Vedas, mathematics, astronomy, painting and sculpture, music, the spinning and weaving sections were all visited. The last department was that of philosophy and political science.

'Alexander met Chanakya, a teacher of political science. Their encounter was less than friendly.

'"Do you know our philosopher Aristotle, who is a master of philosophy?" Alexander asked Chanakya. "We are fairly advanced in this field and my teacher was Aristotle," he added.

'Chanakya was not receptive to this. Omphis told him, "You know, the greatest warrior on earth is here with us. It is a matter of prestige for us. He is going to conquer the world. Haven't you heard of him?"

'"Maybe he does not know much about warriors," said Alexander. "The Brahmin may know about the Vedas and inner peace, but how can he know about external conquests?"

'Chanakya was furious. "If you possess an ability that others do not, do not let it go to your head. Egoism is an anaesthetic that deadens the pain of stupidity. To an egoistic person, the world begins, ends and revolves around him. Success seduces smart people to believe that they will never go wrong. Your defeat awaits you on our soil. You will know reality soon."

"'Arrest him!" ordered Alexander. "This Brahmin does not know to whom he is talking. I want him arrested and brought to my camp straightaway."

'Omphis' commander-in-chief, Devadutta, took Chanakya into custody. Alexander and his troupe returned to their camp.

'But Chanakya escaped from the custody of Devadutta and vanished into the forests. It is a mystery as to how he escaped. Devadutta was beaten in punishment. How did an old Brahmin conquer a commander?'

Samrat Chandragupta just smiled to himself, because he knew how it had happened.

23

'Porus refused to submit to Alexander and hence the Macedonian conquerer began his preparations for war. Alexander tried to learn more about the elephants that would be used in the war. The Greeks camped on the western bank of the Hydaspes river. They could clearly see the mighty army of Porus on the other side of the river.

'It was the monsoon season and the river was swollen with the incessant rains. Alexander decided to distract Porus by engaging in sham encounters, but he had to wait for the waters to recede. It would take a few days. At this time, Kalinos came to Alexander on a secret mission. He told Alexander that he could visit Kurukshetra, the site of the Kuru war, to get clues on the Brahmastra. Ashwathama was willing to accompany them. They embarked on their secret mission by crossing the river quietly without anyone's knowledge. Everyone thought that Alexander was camping on the western bank of the river.

'On their way, Alexander asked Ashwathama, "What is so wonderful about the Brahmastra?"

'"Like other weapons, the Brahmastra is not held in the hands, nor is it usually kept in a quiver like an ordinary arrow. When the need to release this weapon arises, it can be summoned by chanting a mantra. The Brahmastra is released by a mantra derived from the Gayatri mantra. The syllable sounds and pitch may differ from the usual chanting. So, a question arises, what's the difference between those two chants?

Let me tell you that sonic energy is extremely powerful, since it's after all, energy! Any noise made at a particular frequency can destroy objects."

"'If the mantras were recited in particular ways, certain amazing results would take place, including changing the weather, producing certain types of living beings, or even palaces. They can also produce powerful weapons, like the Brahmastra. Specific mantras can be attached to arrows, with the sound causing powerful explosions when the arrow reaches its target. We can also use the science of vibrations to bring our consciousness to higher levels of perception, or to enter spiritual reality.'"

"'The sum and substance of the Brahmastra is this: the Gayatri mantra chanted in a normal manner can have healing and good benefits on a human, but when chanted in a different or varying pitch can turn a *darbha* (a blade of grass) into a Brahmastra!'"

"'There are two types of sound: unstruck/unheard sound (*anahata*) and struck/heard sound (*aahata*). Unstruck is a vibration of ether, the upper or purer air near the celestial realm.'"

"'The enlightened yogis seek the unstruck sound and only they can hear it. The struck sound is a vibration in the lower atmosphere closer to the earth. It is any sound we hear in nature or in man-made forms, musical and non-musical.'"

"'To release the Brahmastra, it is the *anahata* sound which is used to chant the mantra and not the normal *aahata* sound which we use in puja.'"

"'When a person is trained in how to chant the mantra for this purpose, a person has to gain *siddhi* and when he acquires it, he gets energized. With that energy, when he releases even a grass blade by chanting, it turns into the Brahmastra due to his own charged energy and the missile in turn derives its power from Lord Brahma, the creator of this universe! The weapon is also believed to cause severe environmental damage. The land where the weapon is used will become barren and all life in and around the area will cease to exist. Both men and women will become infertile. There will also be a drop in rainfall with the land developing cracks, like during a drought."

'Alexander asked Ashwathama: "Do you know how to summon the Brahmastra?" He replied, "Only Arjuna and I knew of it. But now I have forgotten the method of initiation. I am living now only to regain my knowledge of the Brahmastra, and am joining you to regain that knowledge. I am keen to destroy the lineage of the Pandavas. I initiated the Brahmastra for that purpose after the great war. But due to the intervention of Lord Krishna, one of the sons escaped the onslaught of the Brahmastra and I was cursed to live with this ugly body forever. But I will not let the Pandava lineage continue. Porus, the king of Pauravas, is a descendent of the Pandavas. I was told you are going to war with him. That is why I support you."

"'Ashwathama, you seem to know everything about the past. Do you know anything about amrit?" asked Alexander.

"'Alexander, you know that Hermes Trismegistus was said to have drunk the white drops and thus achieved immortality. The elixir of life is equated with the philosopher's stone, which can grant the drinker eternal life. In our scripture, it is known as amrit. Anybody who consumes even the tiniest portion of amrit has been said to gain immortality. The legend has it at one time, the evil demons gained strength. This was seen as a threat to the demi-gods. So these gods (including Indra the god of sky, Vayu the god of wind, and Agni the god of fire) went to seek advice and help from the three primary gods: Vishnu (the preserver), Brahma (the creator) and Shiva (the destroyer). They said that amrit could only be gained from the *samudra manthan* (or churning of the ocean) since the ocean hid mysterious and secret objects in its depths. Vishnu agreed to take the form of a turtle on whose shell a huge mountain was placed. This mountain was used as a churning pole, and was called Kailash."

"'With the help of a Vasuki, the churning process began at the surface. From one side, the gods pulled the serpent, which had coiled itself around the mountain, and the demons pulled it from the other side. As the churning required immense strength, the demons were persuaded to do the job—they agreed in return for a portion of amrit. Finally, with their combined efforts, the amrit emerged from the depths. All the demi-gods were offered the drink but they managed to trick the demons, who did not get the holy drink."

"'Fierce fighting ensued between demi-gods and demons. The divine bird Garuda took the nectar and flew away in order to protect it. Drops of amrit spilled in four places: Haridwar, Prayag, Trimbak and Ujjain."

"'The oldest Indian writings, the Vedas, contain some hints of alchemy," Kalinos added. "Also mercury, a vital ingredient in alchemy, has been heavily researched by Chanakya, the black Brahmin of Taxila University called "Black" because of his dark complexion. He knows something about the nectar."

'Alexander intervened. "Who? That teacher who escaped my arrest? He seems to be a black magic man. I will not let him go.'"

24

'The next day, they rode around Kurukshetra, the site of the great war. At one spot, the horse suddenly stopped and started digging the earth.

'"What is my horse doing?" asked Alexander. He spoke into the horse's ears.

'Ashwathama intervened. "Alexander, I told you, your horse is the reincarnation of the same horse that was sacrificed during the yagna performed by the Pandavas. Many precious things were placed at its burial site. In fact, Arjuna placed the secrets of the Brahmastra in that very spot, since he felt that the secrets of the Brahmastra should be buried once and for all. Perhaps your horse being the reincarnation of the same horse, is digging in search of the secret you are hunting."

'"Wonderful, my horse brought me to this place with a purpose. Let us wait and see," Alexander replied.

'While they had been talking, the horse dug up a seal with inscriptions on it. The writings were not clear. The men removed the mud from the plate and tried to read what had been written.

तं भूसुतामुक्तमुदारहासं वन्दे यतो भव्यभर्व दयाश्री:।
श्रीयादवं भव्यभतोयदेवं संहारदमुक्तमुगसुभूतम् ॥

आर्दिआ　　　　　आर्दिआ　　　　　आर्दिआ

यदा अमृतलोके प्रथम अष्ट कुञ्चिका;
प्रतिष्ठापयेत् तदा यो विनाशक.
तूष्णीम् द्वाविंश रत्नानि रक्षयति
स्व दूत प्रति अस्त्राणाम् मतेति
वर्तभानम् नवम् कुञ्चिका ज्ञानपयेत्

'The destroyer silently guarding twenty-two jewels will unravel the ninth key, the mother of all missiles through his messenger, once the first eight keys from the land of amrit are located.'

"'Ashwathama, I do not make anything of this. It's a jumble of symbols and text. What language is this? The reference to twenty-two jewels…I know that the Hebrew language has twenty-two alphabets. The magic Greek cube has twenty-two faces. But they have nothing to do with this land. I cannot make head or tail of this message. Is it about the Brahmastra? Is it about amrit, since it refers to land of amrit? You knew the Brahmastra. Can you decode this message?"

"'Alexander, I told you I had been cursed to forget the mantra that could invoke the Brahmastra. This message confuses me, I do not make anything of it." Ashwathama replied.

'Kalinos could not decipher the words either. But the men took the seal back with them as they proceeded towards the Greek camp. At that time, they saw an old man drawing tattoos on the people who passed. There was a huge crowd around him. He was very old but he was highly skilled in tattooing people. Ashwathama took Alexander to him and said to him, "Old man, you know the conqueror of the world—Alexander— admires your skills. Can you do a tattoo on his palm?"

'The old man looked up. "The conqueror of the world wants a tattoo from me? That's strange. But I should inscribe some tattoo that is memorable and worthy of a world conqueror. Do you have any symbol in mind?"

'Kalinos had an excellent idea. "Can you inscribe the exact symbols and message that is on this seal?" He showed him the seal they had found.

'"Why not?" The old man created a tattoo that was an exact replica of the images on the seal.

'"Sir, even if the seal is lost, the secret we have unearthed will be permanently on your body. We can decode it once we finish the war with Porus," Kalinos said.

'They were all very happy to have found a clue. While they prepared to leave, the old man remarked, "The Black Brahmin of Taxila University is the only man who can decode this mysterious language."

'On hearing this, Alexander looked at both Kalinos and Ashwathama. They did not exchange any words.'

25

Helen's story continued as follows.

'On their way back to the war front at Hydaspes, Alexander asked the other two, "The old Black Brahmin was rebellious while speaking to me. When I ordered his arrest, he escaped. He seems to be knowledgeable in the ancient secrets of your land. He must have done a lot of research at Taxila University."

'"He hails from the southern Malabar region, where they practise black magic. Maybe he knows black magic. We have to be careful with him," Kalinos said.

'"First, let me finish the war with Porus. Then I will address the issue of the Black Brahmin."

'They reached the Hydaspes bank where the army was in a state of readiness. Of course, the seal recovered from Kurukshetra was safely placed in the custody of Alexander.

'Then on a stormy night, Alexander and his troops crossed the Hydaspes. Porus advanced with his whole army to meet Alexander. He had 4,000 horses, 200 elephants, 300 chariots and 30,000 infantry. He stationed his elephants in front, as Alexander did not know how to deal with elephants. The cavalry and chariots were placed on the flanks and the infantry behind the elephants.

'Alexander did not dare to attack the centre as his horses could not face elephants, and his phalanx was not superior to the infantry of Porus. But his cavalry was stronger than the other king's. He attacked Porus on his left wing. Alexander's army showered thousands of missiles at the elephants, which fled and crashed through Porus's own cavalry and infantry, causing terrible injuries. Porus, a seven feet tall giant, fought on till the very last chance for resistance was gone. He was wounded on his left shoulder but stood firm on the battlefield.

'Alexander was impressed by his bravery. He sent a message to Porus and met him. Porus was not broken by the defeat and he came there as one brave man meets other.

'"Your age has not deterred your fighting spirit," said Alexander.

'"Alexander, deep roots are not reached by frost. The old that is strong does not wither," Porus looked into the eyes of Alexander and spoke. Impressed by his bravery, Alexander asked him how he should be treated. Porus replied, "Treat me, oh Alexander, as befits a king."

'Alexander was pleased with his reply and allowed Porus not only to govern his own kingdom but also promised to add to it a great patch of territory from his future conquests. Porus became an ally of Alexander from then on.

'Then Alexander retired to his camp at Taxila and Omphis offered him a grand reception. Alexander asked Omphis to take him to Taxila University to the room of Chanakya. He broke open the door and searched the room. Omphis did not know what he was searching for there. There were many writings on palm leaves, old seals scattered all over. As Alexander surveyed the room, he saw a table, one of whose legs was made of a cluster of wood pieces, while the other legs were made of single pieces.

'Alexander asked his people to disband the blocks. To his surprise, he found a hollow space within the leg. In that hollow space, a container filled with liquid was visible. It was labelled "Amrit."'

'Alexander was thrilled. He took that container with him and moved on to his camp.

'Ashwathama was waiting for him. Alexander ignored him and went inside. He told Kalinos, "Send this man out. I do not need him anymore. He is more of a nuisance than of any use to us. We have got what we wanted. Decoding the seal to unlock the secrets of Brahmastra can be done later. Anyway, he is not familiar with the secret and he forgot all the mantras for the initiation of the Brahmastra. Moreover, many of my men want to go home, rest for a while and then come back. I am not marching east towards the Nanda kingdom. Let me give rest to our people, relax and come back. Now that the clues are with us, our mission has been accomplished."

'Ashwathama overheard this. He was unhappy that Alexander and Porus had entered into a truce. He had been deprived of his revenge. His displeasure with Alexander grew when he overheard this. "Traitor, let me see how he can access amrit and the Brahmastra without me. Let me leave him. I will join the Black Brahmin and find ways to eliminate Porus and discover the Brahmastra again. I will never see this barbarian again." Saying this, Ashwathama left.'

26

This is how Helen's story went on:

'The next morning, Alexander spent some quiet time alone with his horse. He had the habit of talking into the horse's ears. Both had their ways of understanding each other.

"'Ambrosia! Ambrosia! Bucephalus, my dear horse, we have ambrosia. We are going to live forever. Look at this container. This has ambrosia. Let us drink this and live forever."

'He gave half of the liquid to the horse and drank the rest. He was very happy. During the day he spoke to his generals about his plans to return to Macedonia.

'That evening, his horse collapsed. He called the doctors, and even asked Kalinos to bring some local physicians. They checked and declared that the horse was dead. It seemed to have been poisoned. Alexander was furious. He told Kalinos about the ambrosia. He did not know whether the Black Brahmin had tricked him into drinking some poison instead of amrit.

'But Kalinos consoled him. "Alexander, since the Black Brahmin hid it, it must have been amrit. Do not worry. But sometimes, amrit can work negatively on animals. It will do its work on you. Don't worry."

"'Kalinos, I have to give my horse royal honours. He has stood by me through all my battles, and was my best companion. No human has been as close to me as Bucephalus. I want to build a memorial for my horse. I want to name a city after him, and I want to go back to my country in this week." Alexander, the conquerer of the known world, sobbed. Emotions cannot be conquered even by an emperor, Kalinos thought. Omphis was asked to allot a site on the western bank of the Hydaspes. A new city, Bucephala, was founded the next day. Devadutta, the commander of Omphis, was put in charge of building it.

'A tomb was erected and a building was constructed with the statute of a horse. That night, Alexander wanted to spend time with his horse in the graveyard. Left to himself, Alexander cut the Brahmastra seal into four equal pieces and attached each one to each leg of the horse who was to be buried. This was done to hide the secrets. He loaded all the bounty—gold, silver and ornaments, diamonds—into the horse's tomb. The next day, the tomb was sealed and an engraving was placed over it. It read, "The closest friend of King Alexander, Bucephalus, lies here peacefully. This is the last place where Alexander halted his campaign".

'Alexander appointed satraps to rule the countries he had conquered and gave responsibilities to Porus and Omphis to rule in his name. After making all the arrangements, Alexander was ready to start his journey.

'Just before embarking on his journey, he wanted to have a last glimpse of the horse that had been buried. He could not get his mind off his horse. That night, he went alone to the tomb, opened the cover and looked inside.

'To his shock, Bucephalus's legs were missing. The bounty had been stolen too. Alexander was very angry. Who could have done this?

'He thought it better not to announce what had happened, as it would bring him shame. When he walked away from the tomb, he had tears in his eyes. He was truly alone now.

'The return march was one of hardship. At the mouth of the Indus, Alexander sent the fleet to sail along the coast and up the Persian Gulf, while he led the land forces towards Susa and Babylon. The men suffered dreadfully and Alexander shared their sufferings.

'Shortly after reaching Babylon, he was attacked by fever. Alexander knew it was the result of the same drink that had killed his horse. It was too late for him to be saved; the Black Brahmin Chanakya had successfully sprung his trap.

'Alexander's generals gathered around the deathbed. They asked him whom he wished to succeed him. He drew his signet ring from his finger and said, "To the strongest". He called Seleukos, one of his generals, and told him about the loss of bounty and the loss of the seal leading to the Brahmastra. He had the same tattoo made on Seleukos's palm. He told him to take over the territory of Persia, up to the Indus. He also asked him to bring the Brahmastra and amrit to Macedonia. Then, he took his last breath.

27

The events after Alexander's death were of follows:

'While the royal guard of honour buried Alexander's mortal remains, Seleukos began the mission he had been assigned. He sent special emissaries with the image of the tattoo, the replica of the seal, and asked them to follow the clues and identify the secrets of the Brahmastra. They were also to look for those who had looted the bounty from the grave of Alexander's horse.

'These emissaries went back to Taxila, and discussed their mission with Omphis. The decoding of such an old seal was not an easy process. Omphis thought he would involve Ashwathama, the wandering man who knew about the Brahmastra. He sent word for him. Ashwathama laughed when he heard the whole story. "I told Alexander he cannot find it by himself as the deep roots of Bharat should be familiar to the decoder. He actually left me, once I helped him get the clues. Why should I help his people now?" he asked.

'"Whatever you want, we will do," Omphis said.

'"I want ownership of the Brahmastra and only on my orders can it be used. Once the Brahmastra is identified, the descendant of the Pandavas, Porus, has to be unseated." These were Ashwathama's demands.

'Omphis agreed to them, along with Philip, the satrap of Alexander. A deed was written and given to Ashwathama.

'The tattoo, the replica of the seal, was shown to him. He took a close look at it. He asked Omphi what he thought the clue could mean.

"'It could be anything. It could be the map to the underground tunnels of the Bharthari caves that link the four ancient dhams of worship of Lord Shiva and Lord Krishna. It could lead to the place that hosts the secret of immortality—the Amarnath caves. Lord Shiva revealed the secret to Parvati at the Amarnath caves. Once, Parvati urged Shiva to tell her the secret of immortality. He kept postponing his reply, but she was adamant to know. Finally, Shiva selected the Amarnath cave where the secret of immortality could not be heard by anyone else. Reaching the cave was not easy. Shiva decided to leave all his belongings behind before entering the cave. During his journey, he asked Nandi the bull to wait for him and he proceeded towards the cave. That place is known as Pahalgam. At the second stop, he removed Chandrama (the moon) from his head. This place got the name Chandanwari. At the third stop he left his snakes and the place got the name Sheshnaag. Even today, the lake of Sheshnaag is green in colour and at night one can see the reflection of the precious Naagmani on its surface. At the next stop, he left his son, Ganesha, so the place got the name Mahagunus Parvat. At the fifth halt, Panchtarni, he left the *panchtatav* (the five elements of creation). Finally, he reached the cave. Lord Shiva began telling the Amar Katha to Parvati. But before the completion of the story, she felt asleep. Incidentally, two birds were listening to the story at that time. As a result, they become immortal. Even today, the two birds can be spotted near the holy cave. Here Lord Shiva is present in the form of a shivling made of ice. This shivling forms during the waxing moon and reduces during the waning moon. We can locate those birds at Amarnath and learn about the secrets of immortality.'"

Amarnath caves
Photo: Wikimedia Commons/Gktambe

Amarnath caves
Photo: Wikimedia Commons/Gktambe

"'Ambhi, stop right now. We have to read the seal, decode the symbols. We cannot speculate based on our knowledge of the location of amrit. We need to decode the seal first. It seems these are several Indus scripts and symbols which were in use 10,000 years ago. I think Rishi Vyasa must have written it for Arjuna. The civilization went underneath the ground during the massive earthquake in that region. The script remains a mystery, and it will remain so. Only Rishi Vyasa may decode it. Where can we find him now?"

'Ashwathama continued. "I can only read the lines in Sanskrit. It says the destroyer is silently guarding twenty-two jewels. It refers to Lord Shiva, but in which location? What are the twenty-two jewels?" Ashwathama pondered over this. "Further, here is the poem on the seal. The striking feature is that the second line is always the reverse of the first:

तं भूसुतामुक्तमुदारहासं वन्दे यतो भव्यभवं दयाश्री:।
श्रीयादवं भव्यभतोयदेवं संहारदामुक्तमुतासुभूतम्।।"

"'The last line addressed to Krishna reads like this:

भव्यभतोयदेवं संहारढामुक्तमिू उत असुभूतं श्रीयाढवं वन्दे।"

"'It means this:

' "I bow down before Krishna, the descendant of the Yadava family, who is the Lord of the sun as well as the moon, and who is the soul of this entire universe."

"'Now there is a reference to Krishna and Shiva. This means we have to look at the places where Shiva was worshipped at the time of Krishna, during the Kuru war."

"'I can think of only one occasion. Krishna advised Arjuna to pray to Lord Shiva for weapons. Arjuna went to Kailash and started worshipping Lord Shiva. We need to go to Mount

Kailash, that is the place referred to on this seal. The message refers to "the destroyer", that is, Rudra. You know I am the partial incarnation of Lord Shiva and I am the twelfth Rudra. The message decodification and the unlocking of secrets can only be done through Rudra."

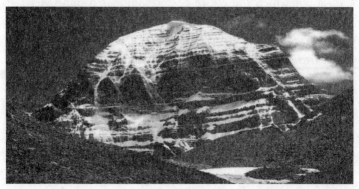

Mount Kailash
Photo: Wikimedia Commons/Ondrej Zvacek

'It was an amazingly symmetrical 22,000-foot striated pyramid with a diagonal gash on one of its faces. The number 22,000 seemed to indicate something the twenty-two jewels referred to in the seal. This thought crossed their minds. Ashwathama explained its significance to Philip.

'In Indian mythology, Mount Mandara is the cosmic pivot around which the serpent was twisted in order to churn the Sea of Milk at the beginning of time. By alternately tugging at either end of the coil, demi-gods and demons managed to extract amrit, the nectar of immortality. The process also gave rise to butter, the sun horse and the wish-fulfilling tree. This mountain is known as Mount Kailash or Mount Meru. It serves as the ladder that links heaven and earth.

"'This pivot is at the very centre of the celestial arrangement. It marks the spot about which the equinoxes move. In other words, the Sea of Milk is the Milky Way, and every 20,000 years or so, the path of the entire solar system wobbles as does the handle of a top. The point or very tip, that is, the spot about which the entire cosmos spins is Mount Meru."

"This must be the place where we will get the answers. It has the amrit reference and the Brahmastra reference. We should check this place thoroughly." Philip sounded very confident.

"'Kailash is one of the most mysterious and wonderful places on earth, where Lord Shiva resides with his wife Parvati. It is called the jewel of snow. It is the centre of the universe." Ashwathama went on. "Lord Shiva, the destroyer of ignorance and illusion, resides at the summit of this legendary mountain, where he sits in a state of perpetual meditation along with his wife Parvati."

"'Now let me come to the puzzle of twenty-two. According to the Puranas:

• Mount Kailash has	4	faces (crystal, ruby, gold and lapis lazuli)
• Located at the heart of	6	mountain ranges symbolizing the lotus
• From it flows	4	rivers (Brahmaputra, Karnali/Ganga, Sutlej and Indus)
• These rivers stretch to	4	quarters of the world
• Holy centre of	4	religions (Hinduism, Buddhism, Jainism and Bon)
• Total	twenty-two	

'"See, twenty-two features are attributable to this mountain where Shiva is meditating. Therefore, there is no doubt the clue of the Brahmastra leads to Mount Kailash. We will spend thirty days surveying this place and talking to the various sadhus here to locate what we want."

'Then, for the next thirty days, they searched and talked to various people, but there was no result. Satrap Philip gave up the expedition and went home. Philip wrote to Seleukos, "Very few people will admit the failure as emanating from the choices they made, but I admit it. We engaged the best pundits to decode the seal, went ahead according to their interpretations, but ended up with failure. We will give up this mission and focus on territorial expansion." He passed the message on to Seleukos, saying that there was no point in wasting time on this, as the efforts were leading to no results.'

Finally, Helen's story came to an end. 'Samrat Maurya, give me some time for love. I am longing to hug you.' Samrat obliged, giving her a passionate kiss.

'That means you gave up on Alexander's expedition to find amrit and the Brahmastra?'

'Samrat, the creator expects each one to do what one is capable of at any point of time. He does not expect an ant to haul timber like the elephant in a forest. The ant should not compare itself to an elephant and start complaining. We aborted our attempts to find these treasures once and for all. Now Samrat, let us begin the war of love. But once we start, it will be very hard to stop me. My desire to physically conquer you through my love is insatiable, Samrat. Come on, let us not waste time.'

'But one thing, Samrat. I told you my full story, therefore,

I will not let you go until you tell me about yourself, from where you originated and how you managed to end the Nanda empire even though you had very few resources.'

PART IV

Rudra Recalls

28

Back at the Massaga fort, Swastika was still in the honeymoon phase with Rudra. She still called him Commander despite repeated requests from Rudra not to do so. For her, the name brought back to her the complete memory of how they had got married.

Rudra accepted her story, and Swastika's mad love for him continued unabated. Swastika asked Rudra, 'Commander, you have not told me anything about yourself. None of your colleagues seem to know you well. Why this veil of secrecy, Commander?'

'What do you want to know?' asked Rudra.

'Commander, your birth, your rise to power at a relatively young age—all this and much more. I must know you, as your wife. Is that not true?'

'Yes, Swastika. But I do not reveal the details of my personal life to anyone. I am telling you on your request, but on the condition that you keep everything confidential. I prefer confidentiality since I hold the position of the chief commander of the Mauryan empire,' Rudra answered.

'It will be done, Commander. What you tell me now will be buried in the secret chambers of my soul. It can never ever be unearthed by anyone. Happy?' On hearing this, Rudra was satisfied.

'Very well. Shortly before I was born, Taxila faced a severe monsoon. The rivers were flooded. On a rainy day, my father,

Devadutta, the chief commander of King Ambhi, came down to the university to visit Chanakya. They were close friends and met whenever my father escorted the royal princes to their sessions with him.

"'Professor Chanakya," Devadutta said, "I have not been blessed with a child for a long time. My wife Ramba Kumari cries almost every day. We have prayed to every god, performed every ritual that was recommended. Perhaps we will remain childless in this birth."

"'You have opened your conversation with the same subject for the last ten years, ever since we have been friends," Chanakya interjected.

"'If I do not tell you, who else can I tell? You are my closest friend."

"'I am here to listen. Let me give you a lead. You can take it seriously and proceed with this option. I come from the Malabar region. I am familiar with some of the temples there, where people go with their prayers for children. The key temple with a high success rate is that of Tirupullani—have you heard of it?"

"No," replied Devadutta.

"'Listen, Devadutta, travelling along the coastal stretch of the south between Ramanathapuram and Rameswaram is almost like walking through the pages of the Ramayana. Along the Sethukarai or the bank of the bridge, myth and history combine to give legend new dimensions through ancient shrines, mystic bathing spots and majestic temples. This place attracts thousands of pilgrims. The bridge was built by the monkey army. Lord Rama used this bridge to cross to Lanka to bring back Sita. On this Sethukarai is located the Tirupullani temple in a place called Pullaranyam."

"'According to legend, Pullaranyam was a marshy land full of the sacred darbha grass. Under a peepal tree here, Vishnu appeared before Pula Maharishi in the form of Adi Jagannatha and told him he would be reborn as Rama to cleanse the land of evil. Many years later, when Rama arrived in search of Sita, he came upon a seemingly impassable barrier: the ocean. Tired, Rama lay down on a bed of darbha and sank into deep meditation for three days. Adi Jagannatha appeared and blessed him. Inspired by this, Rama requested Varuna, the water god, to make a path for him.'

"'The Tirupullani temple has a mysterious grandeur about it. Thousands of childless couples do *nagaprathishta* (installing statues of the snake god) at the peepal grove where Adi Jagannatha is supposed to have first appeared. They flock to the temple to drink the *payasam* which is believed to have the same magical properties as the one which Rama's father, King Dasaratha, once gave his childless wives. The most striking shrine in this huge temple is the one with the exquisitely carved figure of Rama lying on a bed of darbha grass.'

"'Adi Sethu, the primary sacred bathing spot along this coast, lies close to this space. Rama is believed to have bathed here before starting work on the bridge and once again on his return. Legend also says Rama and Sita paused over the temple while returning in the *pushpaka vimanam*.'

"'This temple showed the way for Lord Rama. This is the place you should go to. Don't keep complaining about your grievances of not having children. Organize yourself but do not agonize. You should have belief in our traditions, Devadutta. When in doubt, your strong belief will steer you. Go there immediately. Next year you will have your son.'

"'Chanakya, I used to say that God is not present in

idols. Your feelings are your God. The soul is your temple. But this time I have to try to seek God's boon. This time, I will follow your advice, Chanakya. I am going to the temple near Rameswaram, as suggested by you," Devadutta declared.'

29

The story continued as follows:

'Devadutta and his wife Ramba Kumari were on their way to Tirupullani temple, near Rameswaram. Devadutta took a leave of absence from his duty for fifteen days and proceeded south.

'They travelled on their horses for three consecutive days and still they had to travel one more day to reach the temple. They were tired and wanted to rest on their way.

'After a while, they came upon a small gathering of huts. It looked like the ashram of a saint. They went in to seek shelter for the night. When they entered, a voice greeted them.

"Welcome to the land of Siddhas, the land of alchemy and the elixir of life. You have come to the right land in search of your son, who will be born to meet five of the eight Chiranjivis and search for the alchemy of elixir, on which I have written books. He will be there in this world for thirty years only during which he will make an indelible mark on this land. You may find fault with him but the land will respect him forever for the deeds he will perform. The clouds of suspicion may hang over him briefly, but he will always be remembered for his greatest contribution to this spiritual land. God bless you, your prayers will be granted by the lord of Tirupullani and Rameswaram."

'Devadutta was stunned to hear this. He had not even told these people why he had come. But the sage was spot on. Devadutta asked permission to stay the night, and it was granted. One of the assistants of the sage took him and his wife to a small room.

'Devadutta asked the assistant, "Who is this sage?"

"'Sir, he is the holy Shree, Konganar Siddha, the Rishi of the south. He is the son of Bhogar Siddha of Palani and has written more than forty books on alchemy and the elixir of life. He has also contributed treatises on philosophy, medicine and spiritual practices. He predicts the future for some devotees. You seem to be one among them because he predicted it for you on your first visit."

"'Yes, yes, he correctly saw the purpose of my trip. I think he is a mind reader. His prediction skills are remarkable," replied Devadutta. The short life of his prospective son bothered him. He thought he would have a darshan with the sage the next morning and ask more about it. With this thought, he went to sleep.'

30

'The next day, Devadutta wanted to bid farewell to the sage before leaving for the temple.

"'I seek your blessings, Swamiji. Yesterday, you said something about my son," Devadutta started the conversation.'

"'Yes, you will have a son. Name him Rudra; he will destroy all the evils. He will be born in the month of Chitra, next year on the Ardra star. He will be fortunate to receive the guidance of five Chiranjivis."

"'The last incarnation of the Supreme Lord will begin at the end of the current great cycle. There will be so much sin in the world that truth and virtue will not be found anywhere. There will be nothing left to do but destroy this world completely, to make way for the new world that shall begin the next great cycle."

"'At this time, Lord Vishnu will incarnate as Kalki, who will come riding on a snow-white horse called Devadutta, brandishing a flaming comet-like sword, intent on eradicating the reign of evil, vanquishing Yama, reconciling all opposites, renewing the processes of the dharma (paths of virtue), of creation, and establishing a reign of righteousness."

"'Lord Vishnu will take birth in the home of Vishnuyash and Sumati on a bright fortnight of the lunar month of Vaishakh on the twelfth day, in the mystical city of Shambhala. This village will appear in the later part of Kali Yuga in Dakshin Bharat. All the Chiranjivis will then assemble there and Kalki will start his training under one of them, Guru Parashuram. After his training, he will begin a penance to please Lord Shiva and receive as a benediction the divine winged steed Devadutta, the celestial parrot Shuka and the Ratna-Maru sword."

"'Kalki will then marry Padma, the incarnation of Lakshmi and perform the Ashwamedh yagna to begin his process of destruction. A final battle will ensue with the dark forces of the demon Kali on one side and the forces of Kalki and Dharma on the other. After vanquishing the demonic hordes, the lord will usher in the next golden age or Satya Yuga and rule as the King of Shambhala for a 1,000 years before leaving for his abode again."

"'This is the only incarnation of Lord Vishnu that is yet to take place in the present great cycle. He will re-establish righteousness upon earth, and the minds of those who live at the end of the Kali Yuga shall be awakened, and he shall be as pellucid as crystal."

"'The men who are, thus, changed by virtue of that peculiar time shall be as the seeds of human beings, and shall give birth to a race that shall follow the laws of the Krita age (or age of purity)." As it is said: "when the sun and moon, and (the lunar asterism), Tishya, and the planet Jupiter are in one mansion, the Krita age shall return." This is what Bhagavatam says.

"'We have more than 432,000 years for this. But your son will be only one who will get the guidance of five Chiranjivis before the Kalki avatar of Lord Vishnu. Also note that he will have extraordinary mystical powers on land as he is the Bhoomi Putra."

'Keenly listening to Swamiji, Devadutta said:

"Swamiji, you are saying he will live only for thirty years. That is causing me distress."

"'You are facing destiny, not chasing it on your own terms. Destiny is the outcome of your past karmas. In his last birth, he was cursed by his Guruji to lead a short life in future births. Based on the time of the birth of your son, I could infer this prediction from the planetary positions.'

"'The science of such predictive astrology is based on the principle of the evolution of time. The accumulated results of our past lives are brought to the present. The human ego has undergone many previous births and still has to pass through many incarnations before it can become one with the Supreme Being. In the course of its evolution, it seeks higher or lower forms of terrestrial existence, according to the good or bad deeds (karma) of its previous birth. Planets indicate the results of our past actions and the science of astrology defines our future.'

"'The moment one is born into this world, the strong force of the planets starts to control one. Thereafter, the planetary movements and the newborn's movements go in tandem. This is the law of the universe. From the position of the planets at the time of birth, the future of the newborn can be predicted. In expectation of the forthcoming occurrences, we have to proceed with the present. We are driven by nine planets.'

"'Predictive astrology is your guide to destiny. However, your fate is in your hands. The scriptures guide us by telling us what is good and what is bad; what to do and what not to do; how to do and how not to do. Fate is like a game of cards in which you cannot influence the cards that are thrown at you, but how to play them is in your hands. You may get good cards but if you play badly, you will lose, and you may get bad cards and still win if you play carefully. The roadmap is to give you direction but it is you who should take the right turns at the right times!

"'Perhaps you can hand your son over to an excellent Guru in this birth at an early age so that the Guru's curse of the past can be partly undone by the patronage of the Guru of this birth.

"'I can only predict what I see and I have no solutions to alter it. But by the way, whether it is thirty or sixty or ninety years on this planet, it is insignificant. You know the universe has a long way to go.

- Brahma's one night and one day has 1,000 Chatur Yugas each
- His one day is called one Kalpa
- One Kalpa has 1,000 Chatur Yugas
- One Chatur Yuga has four yugas
- Four yugas have 4,320,000 years
- Satya: 1,728,000 years (Four times of Kali Yuga)
- Treta: 1,296,000 years (Three times of Kali Yuga)
- Dwapara: 864,000 years (Two times of Kali Yuga)
- Kali: 432,000 years (one)

"'We have yet to complete 540 Chatur Yugas that is 540 × 4,320,000 years left. That is a huge number of years!

"'The cycles are repeated like the seasons, waxing and waning within a greater cycle of creation and destruction. Against this, you live thirty or sixty or ninety years, none of them are significant. Be happy with what you have."

"Swamiji, what will be his future?" the ever inquisitive Devadutta continued.

"I can only tell you what I can predict. I cannot give day-to-day predictions. Life is like navigating in uncharted territory. There is no charm in knowing everything in advance. Further, it is only the Almighty who knows, we are all messengers—we can say what we know. All that I can say is this—in his short life, he will make a deep mark on his society and people will remember him for his services long after his demise. You can proceed on your pilgrimage. Best wishes."

'Hearing this, Devadutta moved forward on his pilgrimage to Sethukarai, the Tirupullani temple, praying for the birth of a son.'

31

Devadutta came to Tirupullani, had a darshan and had the *payasam* (sweet dish) served there as *prasadam* for childless couples. Then he went back to Taxila. With the grace of God, Ramba Kumari became pregnant within six months.

'I was born in (330 BC) the next year in the month of Chitra in the Ardra star, as predicted by the Siddha (Tamil sage).'

'I was born to my father Devadutta and my mother Ramba Kumari—this is my birth story. Enough?' Rudra heaved a sigh of relief.

'Oh, no! You have just begun, tell me more after that', Swastika persisted.

'No, worries, I will narrate more', Rudra pacified her.

'Till the age of three, I was not speaking at all. During the third year of my birth I got one more companion in our family, my younger brother—Mudra. My parents were worried about my inability to speak. They thought that I was dumb. My brother started talking from the age of one, and I continued to struggle for words till I was four'.

'My father went to Chanakya, and told him:

"Chanakya, this boy Rudra was predicted to possess great mystical powers and expected to make a deep mark in the world. But he is giving very conflicting signs. I can see his gift or prowess or *vardaan* or whatever you want to call it in his affinity with Mother Earth."

"'I have heard about a miraculous boy through my sources.

Is he the same one? What has this boy done?" asked Chanakya.

"'Guru Chanakya, when he was a baby of just three months, my wife left him on the platform around the tree in our compound. It is of a good height from the ground. She had turned to look at a yachak who had come to the door. Rudra gave a sudden jerk and fell down from the platform to the ground. My wife's heart almost stopped when she realized what had happened. Strangely, he landed on his back and was smiling at the sky, completely unhurt. My wife swore that when she went to pick him up, she felt as though the ground under him was a soft bed, almost as if Mother Earth wanted to embrace him warmly."

"'Another instance was when we went for short trip to the Gandhari caves. He was just one year old. I have told the world that we stumbled upon the caves by chance but I believe that Rudra knew what he was doing. I still remember his determined crawl towards the bushes a short distance from the path. I picked him up and brought him back three times but the fourth time I myself was not looking closely, and then I realized he had disappeared. We started to call his name and heard a faint laugh coming from behind the bushes. I was astonished to see a cave opening wide enough for a man to pass through and a steep staircase going down. This was a hidden cave not yet discovered far from the main caves. Rudra was crawling down the steep old steps as though it was a slide. I could not see how he was doing it as it was dark, but it would not have been possible even for a child of ten years to navigate those steep steps. That Rudra was doing it was a miracle. You, know what we found in the caves. The Kuru era mudhras and gold coins were stashed there. You yourself saw the plethora of missiles that we found in the cave. All the missiles were useless but we now know that they were mass produced in ancient times.

"'The next instance was just a few days after the Gandhari Hills trip. You remember that the climate was exceptionally cold that winter. We were keeping Rudra inside the house. To keep the house cat from going into the room, my wife locked the door. Rudra felt hungry and he woke up. Unable to open the door he made a tunnel under the walls. It was almost as if the ground was crumbling under his touch and creating a path for him. I myself saw the ground sink near the wall and out came Rudra, smiling.

"'The summer months saw us at the riverside in the early morning. I had gone with some of the captains and our families to the riverside for a trip. I along with Rudra and one of my captains with his daughter were walking along the edge. We saw a ledge and sat down while the kids started to go to the sandy area near the edges. Before we knew it, Rukmini, the daughter of the captain, cried out in alarm. A crocodile had come near her and was staring at her. If the crocodile attacked, we had no chance to save her. We were simply too far and the crocodile was too fast. Rudra was some distance away but what he did next surprised us. In anger, he kicked the sand near his feet in the direction of the crocodile. We saw that sandy place tremble, creating a wave. The force was so strong that the crocodile was thrown in the water from the bank, and even Rukmini who was at the edge of the wave, fell down. We ourselves felt the tremors under our feet. The stunned crocodile slunk back in the water. We could understand that Rudra could create an earthquake by playing with the forces beneath the ground.

"'The latest exploit is even more interesting. It is being

studied by the history department at the Taxila University. He dug a huge pit over the course of the evening and unearthed what looked like the tip of a shivlinga. It would have taken me a few days to make a pit of that size by myself. But Rudra could do it in a few hours. Imagine, a toddler could do it with divine intervention. This pit was dig in the corner of the training ground adjoining the palace. The history department is saying that the ruins may be the remains of a temple from the *Treta Yuga* times. They have named it the Rudra temple site and excavations are on."

"'I do not know how he does it. He does these things on his own without any guidance or instruction. We do not know whether he is exercising these powers based on the attributes the Lord has bestowed upon him or these are one-off incidents. Plus, he has not uttered a word till now. He smiles but does not speak even baby gibberish. Is he dumb? Then what is the use of these powers, when the child can't even speak? What can he do in his life? Will his be a wasted talent?"

"'Chanakya, can you take him into your gurukul? You are a man specialized in so many fields, including occult sciences. Only you can make him a man worth something."

"'Devadutta, the cuckoos remain silent for a long time (for several seasons), until they are able to sing sweetly (in the spring) so as to give joy to all. Your boy will speak."

'Devadutta pestered Chanakya to take me into his gurukul.

"What? Have you lost your mind? I am not running a nursery school. What can I do with this child?"

'But he looked deeply into my eyes for a while. I do not know what he thought, but he finally said 'yes' to my father. I went into the gurukul of Chanakya as a young boy of three, perhaps as the last student after Emperor Chandragupta Maurya.

'Interesting indeed!' Swastika exclaimed. 'Tell me about Chanakya, Commander!'

'Chanakya was a professor and economist in Taxila University. He is a Brahmin from Dakshin Bharat. He had tremendous knowledge in various fields, including occult sciences.

'He began his search for a true king when Dhana Nand of the Nanda dynasty insulted him and he was thrown out of the king's court. Chanakya identified our Emperor Chandragupta as a young boy of twelve to thirteen years old, taught him about ruling and warfare and went on to make him the first king of the Maurya dynasty, replacing Dhana Nanda.

'Chanakya had students who respected him and were ready to fight at any moment at his orders. Two of his students— Bhadra Bhatt and Purushdutt—acted as his spies, collecting information from enemies.

'He left the university with the intention of uniting the fragmented kingdoms and saving the country from foreign invaders. I joined this man of high calibre. He always says, "Strategy without tactics may lead you to victory. Tactics without strategy is only the noise." He is the greatest strategist in Bharat.

'I joined him, when he was the university professor. He spotted some potential in me as he did in our Emperor Chandragupta when he was in his teens.

'I was with him from the age of three. With his help, I started speaking and I began to accompany him wherever he went. People used to make fun of him, asking what the child would learn from him. But he had different plans for me.

'He noticed some of my powers and kept me with him. 'When Alexander came to conquer the Bharatiya kingdoms,

Ambhi surrendered to him. He came to Taxila University and had a nasty argument with Chanakya, after which Chanakya was imprisoned. My father, the commander-in-chief of Taxila, was asked to bring Chanakya to Alexander's camp.

'Being close friends, my father asked Chanakya to hit him on the head and allow him to escape to the forest with Chandragupta. Alexander could not understand how a Brahmin professor could escape from the commander-in-chief. He did not know about the deep friendship between my father and Chanakya.'

'Then what happened?' Swastika would not leave Rudra.

32

'Chanakya, Chandragupta and I, the small boy Rudra, were always together. I started speaking clearly and grew in the company of Chanakya. Chanakya was always saying, "Rudra, you are born to achieve. You have special powers given by God. I know how to channelize these powers for our kingdom to be headed by Chandragupta Maurya."

'Chanakya was always asked this question, "How will a small boy contribute to your grand vision?" He used to reply, "Whores don't live in the company of poor men, citizens never support weak company and birds don't build nests on trees that don't bear fruit. Chanakya will keep company with worthy people. Don't bother about the boy's age."'

'He used to counter everyone in his camp who would make fun of me. Once Chanakya thundered—"The elephant has a huge body and is controlled by the *ankusha* (goad), but is the goad as large as the elephant? A lighted candle banishes darkness: is the candle as vast as the darkness? A mountain is broken even by a thunderbolt: is the thunderbolt, therefore, as big as the mountain? No, he whose power prevails is really mighty. This boy Rudra has arrived to make an everlasting impact on our society. You will soon see who this boy is."

'After hearing this, the Chanakya camp stopped making fun of me. From then on, I was also accepted in the company of the adults. Chanakya believed in me. I will ever be grateful to him.'

Swastika intervened. 'Commander, did you learn the sciences from Chanakya?'

'Yes, indeed, observing him was a great way of learning. He used to teach me philosophy at my young age. He would say that as gold is tested in four ways by rubbing, cutting, heating and beating, so a man should be tested by these four things: his renunciation, his conduct, his qualities and his actions. He reminded me of the power of learning. He used to tell me, "Rudra, learning is like a cow of desire. It yields in all seasons. Like a mother, it feeds you on your journey. Therefore, learning is a hidden treasure."

'Chanakya gave me confidence. He used to tell me, "In the world, lots of people will try to grind you down. They need you to be small so that they can be big. You must let them think whatever they want, but you make sure you get your due."

'I grew into my sixth year and then a strange thing happened. One night Chanakya and Chandragupta took me into the place where King Alexander's horse was buried. The place was under the custody of my father, as he was the commander-in-chief of Ambhi, the king of Taxila, who supported King Alexander.

'It was left under my father's control, as Alexander had gone back to his camp since he was in a terrible state of shock after the death of his beloved horse. The horse and Alexander were inseparable. The horse had won him many wars.

'Chanakya asked me, "Rudra, you possess extraordinary skills in relation to Mother Earth. Can you open the grave and then close it the same way after we have finished? No traces of opening or closing should be left."

'I went near the grave. I shook the bottom layer of the grave and opened it with my special skills. Chanakya looked at the buried horse. To our surprise, he looked at the four legs. Four seals were nailed to the legs. Chanakya asked Chandragupta to pull out the seals and the huge bounty of gold, silver and diamonds looted by Alexander. Chandragupta asked Chanakya at that hour, "Do you want us to loot this wealth, once looted by Yavanas (Greeks)? Are you sure, master?"

"'A person should not be too honest. Straight trees are cut first and honest people are harmed first. Our kings who lost to Alexander were straight trees and were looted. We take back this wealth plundered from our kingdoms to re-establish 'Bharatvarsha,' Chandragupta; do not delay your work further."

'At that time we heard some noises. Chanakya ordered Chandragupta to quickly cut the four legs to avoid our being noticed by Alexander's soldiers, who were coming towards the grave.

"'Come on, quick," Chanakya ordered. He took away the four legs of the horse with the seals. I immediately closed the grave, so that it looked the same as before.

'We quickly moved to our forest camp. Under the lamps, Chanakya looked at the four seals. "Oh, the main seal is broken into four parts and pinned with the four legs of the horses as the seals were hidden from the eyes of the people. To keep the seal hidden from the public eye, Alexander did this. Chandragupta, remove the seals from the legs and throw away the legs," Chanakya ordered.

'Then Chanakya assembled the broken seals into different combinations and finally assembled it as one full seal.'

तं भूसुतामुक्तमुदारहासं वन्दे यतो भव्यभर्व दयाश्री:।
श्रीयादवं भव्यभतोयदेवं संहारदामुक्तमुगसुभूतम्॥

आर्दिआ   आर्दिआ   आर्दिआ

यदा अमृतलोके प्रथम अष्ट कुञ्चिका ;
प्रतिष्ठापयेत् तदा यो विनाशक।
तूष्णीम् द्वाविंश रत्नानि रक्षयति
स्व दूत प्रति अस्त्राणाम् मतेति
वर्तमानम् नवम् कुञ्चिका ज्ञानपयेत्

'Interesting, Commander. What did that seal say?' The excitement of Swastika was unstoppable.

'Swastika, wait. Now the Great Hunt begins. Sleep tonight; we will continue tomorrow.' Saying this, Rudra embraced her tightly and took her to the world of romance.

PART V

The Grand Hunt

33

Chandragupta had taken a break from his duties to enjoy the company of the Greek princess for a few days. Rudra did the same to spend time with Swastika at the Massaga fort. As they gazed upon the beauty of the valley from the top of the fort, Swastika took them back to their conversation.

'What did you do after getting the seal, Commander? My head will explode if I do not hear the full story. Please continue, Commander.'

'Swastika, hearing this in itself is exciting for you. Can you imagine the amount of excitement and thrill that we faced during the operation?' Rudra accelerated her excitement further. He continued the story.

'After Chanakya escaped from Alexander, we shifted our base to a forest camp, away from the hustle and bustle of Taxila.

'We kept the bounty in an underground chamber specially created by me. Here, Chanakya studied the seal. He said, "I cannot make anything of this. There are some symbols and these convey something. I know the Indus script carried symbols for written communication. It was in use more than 10,000 years ago. Again, this was in active use 1,500 years ago when there was an agricultural revolution on the banks of the Sarasvati river. When the river dried, the entire population moved out of that place towards the Ganges. Many of those well-constructed cities were buried under the landslide that followed. This script also went out of use, as people moved out and started using Sanskrit or Prakrit as their medium of communication. Where can we go to find the meanings—tell me, Chandragupta?"

"'But master, something is written in Sanskrit," Chandragupta intervened.

"'Yes, I know, I see the word "Ardra" repeated three times. The word star or Ardra is a palindrome, which is a word that reads the same forward or backward. But I do not know its significance. Why is it stated three times? What does it convey? I am breaking my head," Chanakya said.

"'Master, I was born in the birth star of Ardra, so does that mean I will decode the clues and unlock the secrets? Is it conveyed that way?" I asked.

"'Maybe, who knows? But how will you find out, Rudra?" Chanakya interjected. I giggled. Chanakya went on:

'There are two Sanskrit shlokas. The first one has the entire first verse as a palindrome. The second line is the same as the first line, but in reverse.

तं भूसुतामुक्तमुदारहासं वन्दे यतो भव्यभवं दयाश्री:।
श्रीयादवं भव्यभतोयदेवं संहारदामुक्तमुतासुभूतम्॥

'Look at the shloka. The striking feature is that the second line is always the reverse of the first line.

'The first line addressed to Rama in prose order is this:

भूतुतामुक्ति उदार हासं भव्य भव यतो दयश्री: तं वन्दे

'It means: "I pay my homage to him who released Sita, whose laughter is deep, whose embodiment is grand and from whom mercy and splendour arise everywhere."

'The second line addressed to Krishna is this:

भव्यभतोयदेवं संहारढामुक्तिमू उत असुभूतं श्रीयाढवं वन्दे।

'This means: "I bow down before Krishna, the descendant of the Yadava family, who is the Lord of the sun as well as the moon, who liberated even the person who wanted to bring an end to his life, and who is the soul of this entire universe."

'Now we have reference to Rama and Krishna, I am confused.

'The confusion gets compounded by looking at the second shloka of the seal which refers to Lord Shiva: "The destroyer silently guarding twenty-two jewels will unravel the ninth key, the mother of all missiles through his messenger, once the first eight keys from the land of amrit are located."

'Now, the destroyer refers to Lord Shiva. The three references to Lord Shiva, Rama and Krishna are there, but what are we to infer from this? Does this refer to a place where there is a connection between the three? It is baffling!' Chanakya was a worried man.'

34

'Chanakya continued analysing the puzzle. "The references to Rama and Krishna make me think about the characters who appear in both the Ramayana and Mahabharata. Two characters appear in both. Hanuman teaches a lesson to Bhima about humility by asking him to move his tail. Parashuram blesses the Pandavas. But what do these people have to do with this clue?"

"'Yet another reference to Rama was made in the Mahabharata. When Yudhisthira was upset, his questions were answered by Sage Markandeya, narrating examples of Rama's life. Here we can see Rama and Krishna referred to together. But it leads me nowhere!"

"'Is it the place of Lord Shiva where Krishna asked Arjuna to go and pray for great missiles like Pasupathastra? Their reference leads to Mount Kailash where Lord Shiva resides at 22,000 feet above the ground. He is protecting several rivers and regions. But what do twenty-two jewels mean? Or does it refer to Patal Bhuvaneshwar, the cave city? Caves within caves, steps leading to another, each one a deep secret within. The cave is connected by an underground route to Mount Kailash. The Pandavas proceeded on their last journey in the Himalayas after meditating here in front of Lord Shiva. Does this clue refer to the Patal Bhuvaneshwar caves which are as old as the earth itself?" Chanakya's mind worked in various directions.

'He raised another question. "Does the clue refer to

Rameswaram, located at the southern tip of Dakshin Bharat? According to legend, Prince Rama of Ayodhya landed here and decided to do a Shivling puja to expiate the sin of killing a Brahmin, Ravana. So with his consort Sita, Rama ordered Hanuman to bring the Vishwanath lingam from Kailash. But when the auspicious time began, Sita decided to build a lingam from the sand itself since Hanuman had not reached on time. Thus she finished the lingam and the two worshipped there. Hanuman arrived after that and handed over the Vishwanath lingam to Rama. When Hanuman tried to remove the sand lingam he could not do it. The army was confused about which lingam they should offer their prayers to first. Understanding their plea, Lord Rama ordered that the lingam brought by Hanuman be worshipped first by all devotees and only then could they offer prayers to the one made by Sita. This practice is followed till now."

"'Lord Rama's quiver will always have twenty-two arrows. To remind us of his twenty-two arrows and to house the twenty-two ancient rivers of India, there are twenty-two *theerthams* inside the temple complex. So does the seal refer to Rameswaram? Which of these three is the target?"

"'Master, what are the targets?" I asked.

"'Rudra, Alexander was keen to get the secrets of Bharat—the Brahmastra and amrit, the elixir of life. I was listening to the conversation between Alexander and Ashwathama, the negative Chiranjivi. I am sure the seal leads to the answers. These are my targets."

'Master, who are Chiranjivis? Can we meet them?' I asked.

"'Parashuram, Hanuman, Vyasa, Vibhishan, King Bali, Kripacharya and Ashwathama are the seven Chiranjivis. They will live till the end of the Kali Yuga. Sage Markandeya is eternal; he will be there in all yugas. These Chiranjivis will not be visible to all, they may live in some form or other, and only the Yuga Purush can see them. Only Ashwathama was cursed to live with sickness till the end of Kali Yuga, since he wrongly used the Brahmastra in the last yuga. Hence he is called the negative Chiranjivi; he is visible to many of us.'

'Can I see the Chiranjivis master?' I asked, curious to know.

35

'"Why not? It was predicted at the time of your birth that you would be blessed to meet five Chiranjivis in this karmic outing. You are a Yuga Purush, Rudra."

'How about you, master?' I countered. 'A Yuga Purush is the one who can demystify several truths buried during the last yuga. In my opinion, you are the one who will meet the Chiranjivis. Yuga Veer is the one who will be remembered in this age for his bravery, victories in war, and good governance of his kingdom. Chandragupta may be this Yuga Veer.'

'"A Yuga Guru is the one who will identify and cultivate the Yuga Veer and Yuga Purush. That is me—understand Rudra?" Chanakya said.

'What is the Brahmastra, master,' I carried on questioning him.

'"The Brahmastra is the mother of all missiles. It is a missile which can be used to aim with pinpoint accuracy and it can seek and destroy its target. It works on the vibration of the universe. Since Brahma is the creator of Sanatana Dharma, the Brahmastra was created by him for the purpose of upholding 'dharma' and 'satya' to be used by anyone who wished to destroy an enemy. The target hit by the Brahmastra when projected with its full destructive power will be utterly destroyed. The weapon will also cause severe environmental damage. The land where the weapon was used will become barren and all life around that area will cease to exist, both men and women will become infertile. When invoked, there would be flames, thunder and thousands of meteors would fall accompanied by a trembling of the earth. It has to be used only as a last resort and never in combat. It is a single projectile charged with all the power of the universe. Once invoked, the missile must be discharged. In the history of the world, the missile was used rarely only on the following occasions:

- Maharaj Kaushika (who later became Viswamitra) used it against Maharishi Vashista who swallowed it by a counter-astra.
- Ravana's son Indrajit used it against Rama and Lakshmana. Lakshmana was saved by the Sanjeevani herb brought by Hanuman.
- Lord Rama used it against Ravana.
- In the Mahabharata, Bhishma used the Brahmastra against Guru Parashuram, and a counter-Brahmastra neutralized his weapon.
- In the Kurukshetra war, Karna neutralized a Brahmastra sent by Arjuna with an equal Brahmastra and their collision was catastrophic.
- Ashwathama used this weapon against Arjuna and was cursed by Lord Krishna since he had used it for a wrong cause."

'Master, this is very interesting. We need this missile to create our kingdom. But do such weapons truly exist?' Chandragupta asked.

"'Chandragupta, there were far more powerful weapons used during the Kurukshetra war. Consider this verse:

A powerful vimana hurled a single projectile
Charged with all the power of the universe.
An incandescent column of smoke and flame
As bright as a thousand suns
Rose in all its splendour...
a perpendicular explosion
with its billowing smoke clouds...
...the cloud of smoke
rising after its first explosion
formed into expanding round circles
like the opening of giant parasols...
...it was an unknown weapon,
An iron thunderbolt,
A gigantic messenger of death,
Which reduced to ashes
The entire race of the Vrishnis and the Andhakas.
...The corpses were so burned
As to be unrecognizable.
The hair and nails fell out;
Pottery broke without apparent cause,
And the birds turned white.
After a few hours
All foodstuffs were infected...
...to escape from this fire
The soldiers threw themselves in streams
To wash themselves and their equipment."

"'Such powerful weapons, Viman and the amrit, the elixir of life that can retrieve the destroyed lives are all ancient secrets buried in past. Alexander would have carried these secrets away. But the clues reached our hand. We are destined to shape a unified kingdom. But how do we decode the secrets?"

'Chanakya, a veteran of the ancient *shastras* and occult sciences, would never give up. He thought the only way to succeed in our mission was to visit Kurukshetra and look for clues. He knew Vyasa, the Chiranjivi and the author of Mahabharata, could give us a lead. Vyasa knew all languages: past, present and potential. He could decode the Indus script. But he would not be visible to the common man. How could we locate him?

'We came to the Sthanashwar Mahadev temple in Kurukshetra, and worshipped Lord Shiva. Later in the day, we reached Abhimanyu's palace and spent time there.

'It was afternoon when I came to the holy peepal tree, the living witness to the divine message of the Bhagavad Gita, given by Lord Krishna to Arjuna. The place was serene and I tried to meditate beneath the tree. I was in a deep state of meditation. At that time, a strange thing happened.'

'Swastika, listen to this,' Rudra said.'When I was in deep meditation, I heard a shrieking voice calling me—"Karma Yogi!"'

'I turned around. "Yes, I am calling you a real Karma Yogi. One who first acquires knowledge and then works for the welfare of the people, and thus naturally becomes popular. There is no enemy for such a man, but even if there were, he would be able to vanquish them. His popularity in society increases on account of his success and good deeds. You are destined to be a Karma Yogi, my dear boy. That is why I called you thus," the voice continued.

'"May I ask who you are?" I asked.

'"People call me Sage Veda Vyasa," the voice replied. Now I could see an old man with a long white beard.

'I was shocked. The Chiranjivi, who is not visible to the rest of the world, was visible to me.

'"Listen, my dear boy. I am appearing before you because of your good karma. I have a role to play in this Kali Yuga through you. Later, I will make my second and last appearance at the time of the birth of Kalki. You have come in search of answers to the clues inscribed on the seal. Is that not true?"

'This statement stunned me. How did he know the purpose of my visit?

'"I know you are Rudra, my young boy. Don't think you are small. You are the messenger who will open the gateway to the great secrets of this spiritual land. That is why I chose to speak to you. I have been silently watching developments over the years. I have instructions to speak only to you in this Kali Yuga."

"'I do not have all the answers to the clues you are looking for. But I will lead you towards them. These symbols belong to the Indus script which was first used 10,000 years ago, when people communicated through symbols rather than alphabets. This was also used 1,500 years back by the Indus civilization. The civilization moved towards the Ganga on the drying up of the Sarasvati. They moved to new region and adopted Sanskrit as their language along with the people of those regions, leaving their scripts behind. The vacant cities were buried in the land due to massive landslides over the years."

"'You have the seal which combines the symbols of the Indus script and Sanskrit shlokas. I was the one who buried it along with the horse from the great yagna. Emperor Dharma and Arjuna were there when we took the decision to do this. The secrets of this land had to be protected from invaders, who we knew would intrude into this spiritual land in the Kali Yuga."

"'Now it is time to unlock the secrets to unify this land into Akanda Bharat, and also to enable the Chanakya troupe to defeat the Yavanas coming from outside. I will decode some of the symbols.'"

38

Rudra's story continued.

'After educating me about the symbols, Vyasa concluded, "Rudra, there are some questions for which I do not have an answer. The words written as 'Ardra' implies that the man born under the Ardra birth star will be the messenger who will unlock the secrets. It is you, 'Rudra'. The symbol of the warrior also refers to you. The military officer and priest symbols denote people close to you. The Sanskrit poem has different meanings, depending on which side you read from—left to right or right to left. It has to be read from left to right to receive your clue, since one of the symbols with an animal looks towards the left."

'"The message "the destroyer guarding twenty-two jewels" refers to Rameswaram of Dakshin Bharat, where Rudra (Lord Shiva) the destroyer is guarding twenty-two ponds which symbolize the ancient twenty-two rivers of the land. As far as the reference to "eight keys from the land of amrit," goes, I have no clear answer. You may have to visit the place where Sita entered the earth in her final journey. And the ninth key—it is you, Rudra. That is the message I have for you."

'The voice vanished, and I woke up from my dream. By the time I was ready to go, Guru Chanakya had come looking for me.

'"Rudra, where were you? You were missing...did you sleep under this peepal tree?" he asked.

'Yes, master, I was so tired. I slept for a while but to my

surprise, I saw Sage Veda Vyasa in my dream. He decoded several symbols from the seal. He also told me that I am the ninth key referred to in the message.'

"'I had heard that Sage Vyasa lives near this tree. At the end of the Yuga, Mount Meru may be shaken, at the end of the planet's life cycle "Kalpa," the waters of the seven oceans, may be disturbed, but sages like Veda Vyasa will never deviate from the spiritual path, will never utter anything wrong, even in our dreams. Hence, when he came into your dream and told you something, it must be true. Tell me about the clues he gave you."

'I gave him and Chandragupta the answers I had received in my dream.

Symbols Decoded

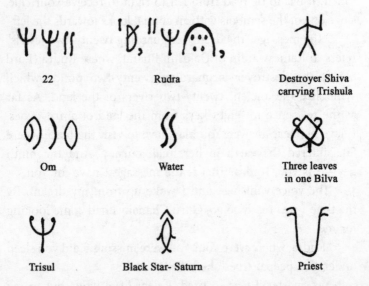

22	Rudra	Destroyer Shiva carrying Trishula
Om	Water	Three leaves in one Bilva
Trisul	Black Star- Saturn	Priest

Warrior

Officer With
military duties

Read from Left to Right as
per the Animals direction

तं भूसुतमुक्तमुदारहास वन्दे यतो भव्यभर्व दयाश्री:।
श्रीयादवं भव्यभतोयदेवं सहारदामुक्तमुग्नसुभूतम् ॥

आर्द्रआ   आर्द्रआ   आर्द्रआ

Ardra refers to Ardra birth star born Rudra

यद्रा अमृतलोके प्रथम अष्ट कुञ्चिका;
प्रतिष्ठापयेत् तदा यो विनाशक.'
तूष्णीम् द्वाविंश रत्नानि रक्षयति
स्व दूत प्रति अस्त्राणाम् मतेति
वर्तभानाम् नवम् कुञ्चिका ज्ञानप्रयेत्

'We sat there, trying to figure out the meaning of the message in light of the new clues. We still had to work through who the eight persons were, who held the keys to the Brahmastra.

'Chanakya continued. "Did he say anything about the unsolved puzzle? Who are the eight keys from the land of Bharat?"

'Master, for the clues, the direction was given to go to the place where Sita entered the earth on her final journey,' I chipped in.

'Chanakya made us get ready at once.'

39

'The place we had to go was Sita Samahit Sthal near Varanasi. Since Chanakya and Chandragupta were on King Dhana Nanda's wanted list, Chanakya had to move about under an assumed identity. He had to grow his hair, remove his tuft and put on the rich attire of a trader. Chandragupta and I also had to match his attire.

'We reached the temple of Mata Sita.

'We spent a few hours there and then all of us retired for the night nearby. But I could not sleep. I went back to the temple. Since it was night, the temple was closed. But I went round the temple. As I am blessed with the skill of reading movements under the earth, I kept my ears to the ground and listened to the sounds for a while.

'I could hear a voice reciting Vishnu's names continuously, even in the middle of the night. It was coming from inside the ground. As I kept my ears closer to the ground, the earth caved in, giving way for my entry. To my surprise, I saw a person dressed in a king's attire reciting prayers to Vishnu. He said to me, "Welcome to Pathala, my dear Rudra. I have been waiting to welcome you in this Kali Yuga. You are thinking, who is this man below the ground in a king's attire? I was the fourth descendant of Hiranyakashyap, and was named Bali. Through my devotion and penance I defeated Indra, the god of the firmament, humbled other gods and extended my authority over the three worlds. All the gods appealed to Lord Vishnu for protection and he became manifest as Vaman for the purpose of restraining me. When I was making a great religious offering, Vaman appeared before me in the company of other Brahmins. I was extremely pleased to see a holy man and promised to give him whatever he should ask for. He asked only for as much land as he could measure with three steps. I laughingly agreed to grant the boon. Lord Vishnu then stepped over heaven in his first stride and the netherworld in the second stride. Then he asked me where he could put his third step. I realized that Vamana was Vishnu incarnate and he was going to take the earth in his third stride. I offered my head. Vamana blessed me, marking me as one of the few immortals blessed by Vishnu. Then out of respect for my kindness and my grandfather Prahlad's great virtues, he made me the ruler of Pathala. I control this region as an immortal Chiranjivi till the end of this Kali Yuga. What were you looking here? Amrit?"

'Yes, we have been guided by Veda Vyasa to look for the missing clue, the references to the land of amrit.'

'He replied, "In the four places of our ancient Bharat, four drops of amrit fell when a war broke out between demi-gods and demons. But I understand Markandeya Rishi, the Chiranjivi beyond all yugas, made sure that it would not reach the wrong hands. You must go to the place where Rama entered the earth in the Sarayu river. You may get more answers."'

40

'Chanakya decided to go to Ayodhya, which is located on the banks of the Sarayu. He did not want to lose more time unlocking clues. He had to defeat Dhana Nanda, the king of Magadha, to create "Akhanda Bharat" under the rule of Chandragupta Maurya.

'We reached Ayodhya, and came to Gutar Ghatt where Rama is believed to have taken "Jal Samadhi" (leaving the earth for "Baikuntha," the divine abode of Lord Vishnu), by drowning himself once he had completed his duties. It offers a picturesque view of the Sarayu and its green banks and has several ancient temples.

Sarayu river
Photo: Wikimedia/Commons/Vishwaroop2006

'All of us took a dip in the Sarayu. To their surprise, I did not come out of my dip. There was panic for some time. Chanakya calmed Chandragupta and said, "Rudra is a Bhoomi-putra, he will come out after finishing his task. Do not worry."

'In the meantime, I had gone deep into the river to the bottom. I saw a cave beneath the water. There I heard someone reciting, "Om, Tryambakam yajamahe sugandhim pushti-vardhanam Urvarukamiva bandhanan Mrityor mukshiya mamritat."

'I knew this was the powerful Mritunjaya mantra created by Markandeya Rishi to get out of the destiny of a short life conferred upon him. My father had taught it to me when I was three years old, saying that I also had a short life and had to be careful when I reached the age of thirty. Hence I always recited this shloka.

'Curious, I peeped into the cave, and was greeted by this response.

'"Welcome Rudra, Yuga Purush. I am Markandeya Rishi, and have been waiting for you for years. You are the one who holds the key to several secrets of our Bharat, buried in this land for several yugas. You are looking for the eight other keys from the land of amrit. Isn't that so?"

'I could not believe my ears. What a boon has been conferred on me, I thought.'

'"My son, according to the Puranas, at the dawn of creation, gods and the demons started the *samudra manthan*, the churning of the ocean which, it was thought, had infinite wealth. Out of fourteen gems found in the ocean, one was amrit. A sip of this rare nectar was enough to make a person immortal. Therefore, both the gods and demons clamoured for it. The gods entrusted Jayanta, son of Indra, to keep the pitcher in safe custody for the exclusive use of the gods. Shukracharya, the king of demons, ordered the demons to snatch the pitcher from Jayanta. The gods and demons fought a twelve-day battle to gain control of the pitcher. Jayanta had to run from place to place but he paused to rest in twelve places out of which four were on earth. The four places on earth where he rested and where a few drops of nectar spilled over and made the place holy are (Haridwar) Har Ki Pauri, Prayag, Nashik (Godavari Ghat) and Ujjain (Shipra Ghat). Since then, Kumbh Melas have been taking place at one or the other of these four places every twelve years."

'Sage, what happened to the four drops of amrit that fell on earth?'

"'Good question, Rudra. I was the one who would be eternal, linking all the Yugas. I was, therefore, entrusted the task of assembling those four drops so that they did not fall into the wrong hands. I took those four drops and planted them along with Rudraksha seeds on this bank of the Sarayu. The Rudraksha tree bore fruits after five years."

"'This tree gave birth to only one bunch of nine unique Rudrakshas with twenty-two faces. That is unique since usually, the Rudraksha can have one to twenty-one faces. Rudrakshas are used for meditation purposes and to sanctify the mind, body and soul. The word Rudraksha is derived from Rudra (Shiva) and Aksha (eyes). The legend says that once Lord Shiva opened his eyes after a long period of yogic meditation and because of extreme fulfilment, he shed a tear. This single tear grew into the Rudraksha tree. It is believed that by wearing the Rudraksha bead, one can receive the protection of Lord Shiva. Rudraksha is the one that has the ability to wipe out our tears. This twenty-two-faced Rudraksha grown from amrit has the power to lead you further in your quest."

"'In order to protect the nine pieces from reaching wrong hands, I gave eight of them to persons randomly chosen from the four varnas, Brahmin, Kshatriya, Vaishya and Shudra, two to each of these varnas. I did this to encourage diversity of ownership. The eight families worship these Rudraksha beads every day, generation after generation, keeping it in their puja rooms. They do not know the power of the beads. They will know of it only when all of them unite along with the ninth Rudraksha. The time has come to assemble them now."

"'I have been holding onto the ninth Rudraksha, waiting for you. You are the ninth master needed to unlock the secrets of this land. Now, it is yours."

'But Sage, where can I find the other eight?'

Rudrakshas

"'The Purna Kumbh Mela is celebrated at an interval of twelve years on the basis of astrological calculations reflecting the planetary positions that prevailed on the day when the drops of amrit fell on the earth. The festival is a symbol of perpetuity and the liveliness of our culture. People from diverse backgrounds come and bathe in the Ganga."

"'But the most important Kumbh Mela is the "Maha

Kumbh" that takes place every 144 years or after twelve Purna Kumbh Mela. It is held at Prayag at the Triveni Sangam, the confluence of the Ganga, Yamuna and the Sarasvati. This Maha Kumbh Mela is going to be celebrated next month in Prayag. There, you will find your eight companions with the twenty-two-faced Rudraksha."

"'Don't worry about how to find them in the huge crowd. I will give you a solution. On the twenty-second day after the Maha Kumbh Mela, you will see the eight of them assemble and offer their prayers, wearing this Rudraksha. That was the day the Rudraksha was given to them by me. Hence, every 144 years, on this day, they all come and pray. This happens generation after generation."

'But Sage, will I find amrit and immortality?'

"'No, Rudra. You may be the Yuga Purush but this is the Kali Yuga. If you are successful, you will uncover powers beyond your imagination, but only I am truly eternal. The amrit that you may find will no longer work for anyone. It is only me now who can truly create the amrit. I do not know anyone worthy of it in this time. You may know about amrit, Rudra, but you will not be able to use it."

'With this, I took the blessings of Sage Markandeya, who also advised me to continue chanting the Mrityunja mantra in order to extend my life.

'I came back to the banks of the river and relieved the tension of my fellows.'

41

Triveni Sangam, the confluence of the Ganga and the
Yamuna rivers in Prayag
Photo: Wikimedia/commons/puffino

'We all waited for the Maha Kumbh Mela. The day came. People from all over Bharat came and bathed in the Triveni Sangam. Chandragupta and Chanakya continued to be in their camouflaged identity as "traders."

But even though we searched, we could not locate anyone who bore a resemblance to the descriptions given by Sage Markandeya. Since thousands of people visited the mala, we could not find the people we wanted.

'As suggested by the sage, we went to the Triveni Sangam

on the twenty-second day after the Maha Kumbh festival. There was no crowd as most of the people had left.

'The rivers maintain their identity and are visibly different even when they merge in the Triveni Sangam. While the Yamuna is deep, calm and greenish in colour, the Ganga is shallow, forceful and clear. The Sarasvati remains hidden, but people believe that she makes her presence felt underwater.

'We were watching from the banks of the Ganga at Daraganj. We saw eight boys with their parents performing a puja on the platforms erected at the confluence. Each group was busy with its own puja and did not bother with the other groups.

'Guru Chanakya exclaimed, "See there, we have sighted the group. Let us go there." We took a boat and reached the platforms. To our surprise, the eight boys were wearing the Rudraksha beads. They were doing pujas with their fathers.

'Chanakya brought them together and addressed them.

"Do you know me? I am Chanakya Acharya from Taxila University. We are working on a plan to unify Bharat. We need your support."

'The parents of the boys looked at him curiously. "What? Support from us for uniting Bharat? We are not that worthy; we are poor people worrying about day-to-day matters, Acharya. We think you have mistaken our identities."

'"No, no, I know. See the boys standing next to me. One is Chandragupta, who will rule that Akanda Bharat for the next few years, and the other is Rudra, the blessed Yuga Purush who will decode several secrets of our ancient land. He was blessed by the Chiranjivi Markandeya who led us to you. You carry twenty-two-faced Rudrakshas. Am I right? You have been passing this Rudraksha from generation to generation without knowing its significance."

"'See, Rudra has one such unique Rudraksha gifted to him by the great sage. All nine boys who carry this Rudraksha are going to serve the nation in a great way. Parents, believe me and send your boys with me to perform their duty. They will form the "Nava Yuva Sena" supporting Emperor Chandragupta Maurya."

'The parents reluctantly agreed. "These are eight-year-old boys. We agree to leave them in your gurukul. But we have one condition—whenever we want to see them, we must be allowed to meet them. Also, they should not be sent to the battlefront till they are sixteen years old."

'Chanakya agreed. The parents left their sons with him. Chanakya asked all the boys, including me, to get familiarized with each other. The boys introduced themselves as Bhava, Sarva, Isana, Pasupathi, Bhima, Ugra, Mahadeva and Shiva. All of them carried different names of Rudra, Lord Shiva. What a coincidence, Chanakya must have thought.

'Chanakya asked them to pray as a group while wearing the Rudraksha. They took a dip at the Triveni confluence after that and then an unexpected event took place.'

42

'All the boys took a dip as a group, joining hands at the confluence. They reached into the water and suddenly found themselves at a door right under the water. They realized they were the doors of a chamber in the river.

Locked Doors that Open to Voice Commands
Photo: Srirangaminfo.com

'The door had two cobras on it and no nuts, bolts or other latches. The cobras seemed to have been fixed to the door with "Naga Bandham" or "Naga Paasm" mantras. The boys did not know how to open the door of the underwater chamber. I recalled what Chanakya had once taught me. Naga Bandham or Naga Paasm can be undone by chanting the Garuda mantra. I chanted the Garuda mantra and the doors of the chamber opened. All of us went into the underwater chamber. We saw nine golden closed bilva leaves—a set of three bilva leaves embedded within each other. Each of these closed golden bilva leaves were placed on an ornate silver box which had a dry palm leaf inside it.

Writings on dried palm leaves

Bilva leaves

'Each boy took one set of leaves along with the silver box containing the dried palm leaf and came back to the platforms at the confluence.

'We told Chanakya what had happened underwater, and then he took us back to the camp. That night, we examined what we had found.'

43

'On closer examination, Chanakya made various observations. The golden bilva leaves were interlocked with each of the other three leaves of a set, all closed tightly. They were joined together but it was possible that each of these closed bilva leaves could open. He himself tried to open them, but failed.

'Then he examined the dried palm leaves, which contained a message. It turned out to be a puzzle. There were nine dried palm leaves with nine puzzles. There was a blank space for filling up the answer. Perhaps that was the key that could lead to opening the closed bilva leaves.

'Guru Chanakya read out the puzzles.

- Rudra's puzzle was this:

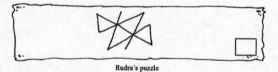

Rudra's puzzle

- Bhava's puzzle:

Bhava's puzzle

- It represents the number of arrows in Lord Rama's quiver (Sarva's puzzle).

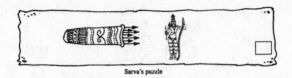

Sarva's puzzle

- It represents the primitive alphabet of all humanity during the period of Lord Rama (Isana's puzzle).

Isana's puzzle

- Symbol (Pasupathi's puzzle).

Pasupati's puzzle

- Symbol (Bhima's puzzle).

Bhima's puzzle

- Avatars of God (Ugra's puzzle).

Ugra's puzzle

- Avatar that killed demons summed up (Mahadeva's puzzle).

Mahadev's puzzle

- It represents the number of ways in which "the number" eight can be partitioned (Shiva's puzzle).

Shiva's puzzle

'The puzzles baffled us. We were confused and dejected at first, but then Chanakya started motivating us.

"'Boys, even cowards can endure hardships, but only the brave can endure suspense. When others are in doubt, your strong belief steers you. Don't worry, and don't complain. Complaining is a sign of weakness. Believe in yourself." The golden words of Chanakya energized us.

'We started pondering over the puzzles one by one. My puzzle, the diagram, could not lead us anywhere. So Bhava's puzzle was taken up.' 'This is the Indus script decoded by Sage Vyasa. Twenty-two is the answer!' I shouted.

'Sarva's puzzle on the number of arrows in Lord Rama's quiver lead to the answer twenty-two again.

'Isana's puzzle on the primitive alphabet of all humanity during the period of Lord Rama stumped us. After considerable thought, Chanakya came up with the answer. Several alphabets had twenty-two letters. The primitive alphabet of all humanity during the period of Rama comprised of twenty-two signs.

'Pasupathi's puzzle was the head of a man. Did it refer

to any particular person? Did it reflect a man of a particular tribe? After several rounds of deliberations, we came up with the answer of twenty-two. The head consists of twenty-two bones, eight for the cranium and fourteen for the face.

'What about the rest?'

44

'Bhima's puzzle consisted of a symbol: the trident, a zodiac sign and a planet.

'Guru Chanakya came to the answer: Trident (3) + Zodiac sign (12) + Planet (7) = 22.

'Ugra's puzzle posed serious problems. It asked about the avatars of God. The avatars of Vishnu were ten, Lord Shiva took birth on the earth as eleven Rudras. But these were not compatible with the rest of the answers which revolved around the number twenty-two. Was there any link between the avatar of God and twenty-two?

'Chanakya came up with the answer. 'The *Mastya Purana*,' he said, 'lists twenty-two avatars of God (*Mastya Purana* 32–52).' Further, he substantiated with the fact that *Srimad Bhagavatham* lists twenty-two avatars of God (Chapters 1–3).

'Mahadev's puzzle referred to the avatars that killed demons. The team could arrive at the solution this way— the Varaha (third avatar), Narasimha (fourth avatar), Rama (seventh avatar) and Krishna (eighth avatar) were the ones who destroyed demons. 3+4+7+8 = 22 (yet again).

'The next was Shiva's puzzle, where everyone fumbled. The puzzle concerned the number of ways the number eight could be partitioned. All of us refrained from suggesting any answer to this, since we had no clues.

'Guru Chanakya said there are twenty-two ways in which the number eight can be partioned. He explained it to us this way:

(8),(7+1),(6+2),(6+1+1),(5+3),(5+2+1),(5+1+1),(4+4),(4+3+1),(4+2+2), (4+2+1),(4+1+1+1+1),(3+3+2),(3+3+1+1),(3+2+2+1),(3+2+1+1+1),(3+1+1+1+1+1),(2+2+2+2),(2+2+2+1+1),(2+2+1+1+1+1),(2+1+1+1+1+1+1),(1+1+1+1+1+1+1+1)

Thus all the eight puzzles other than mine led to the answer of twenty-two.

'Chanakya went into deep thought. He looked at the seal, searching for a clue. He could recall that out of all the symbols on the seal taken from Alexander, only two symbols had not yielded any clue at the time. One was the bilva leaves, and the other, Saturn. Now the bilva leaves had found a place in the decoding process, but what about Saturn (the black star)?

'Was there any relationship between Saturn and the puzzle found on my palm leaf?

'The answer suddenly flashed in his mind at that time. The Saturn magic square!

'A magic square is an array of numbers consisting of the distinct positive numbers arranged so that the sum of numbers in any horizontal, vertical or diagonal number is the same. The Saturn square consists of the first nine digits and any row or column adds up to the number of fifteen. But there are several ways to get this result in a 3/3 magic square. Which one would be the answer to this puzzle?

'But of the different ways to get the same result in a 3/3 magic square, the one that fit the symbol found on my palm leaf was this:

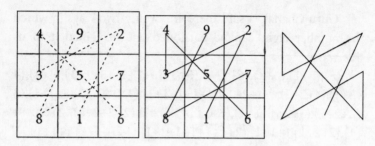

Saturn magic square   *Puzzle symbol*

45

'Guru Chanakya asked the boys to write the answer on their dried palm leaves. Once they did so, an unexpected thing happened.

'The nine golden bilva leaves opened up. Each one contained a letter. What was that?

रा	म	लि	न	गा	य	न	म	ह
Ra	Ma	Li	N	Ga	Ya	Na	Ma	Ha
1	2	3	4	5	6	7	8	9

'Confusion arose! We didn't know what to do with these letters. Did they represent a password for something? Guru Chanakya asked us to recite the word multiple times as a prayer. There was no effect. Was all our effort going to waste?

'The whole team was frustrated. What could we do next? Should we abandon the project?

'Chanakya boosted our morale with his powerful speech. "Boys, small achievements lead to great victories. Opportunity is under your feet. We do not keep brooding on our misfortune. All we need is to recognize that there is an opportunity. Most people complain of noise without knowing that it is opportunity that is knocking at their door. They may recognize the opportunity, but only when it is leaving. We have dug the gold mine for gold and not for dust. We dig the land unmindful of the dust, focusing on the gold. Don't worry about the dust boys, go for the gold! Most people give up at the last minute just a foot away from a win. The only limit to our realization tomorrow will be our doubts of today. Hence, do not doubt yourself. Be positive, boys. A positive mind emits harmonious thoughts, a negative mind discordant ones. A pessimist sees difficulty in every opportunity. An optimist sees opportunity in every difficulty. Be optimists, boys! Your attitude alone determines your altitude."

'Guru Chanakya's words charged us. I replied, "Guruji, we agree many of us are pulled into the ordinary pursuit of life and lose sight of extraordinary opportunities. We trust our inner feelings, and we will have the answers, Guruji. We are confident we will make it happen."

'Guru Chanakya applauded me. "That is the spirit, Rudra. Sail away from the safe shores. Catch the trade winds in your sails. A smooth sea never produces a skilful sailor. There is no wind that always blows. Nothing worthwhile comes without a struggle, and when the world says "give up", hope whispers "Try one more time." The greatest discoveries and philosophical expositions emanate from positive energy. On a day when you don't have a problem, you can be sure that you are travelling along the wrong path. Do not go where the path may lead, go instead where there is no path and leave a trail. An idea can turn into dust or magic depending on the talent that rubs against it. You are all a great bunch of talent, my dear boys, and you will make it. Failure is an option, but fear is not. Come on, boys!"

'Upon hearing this, the whole team was brimming with confidence. At that time, an unexpected thing happened!'

46

'Chandragupta, who had remained a key observer, broke his silence. He said, "Guru Chanakya, if you recall the message of the seal which we took from the grave, it says "the destroyer guarding the twenty-two jewels will unravel the ninth key, the mother of all missiles through his messenger, once the first eight keys from the land of amrit are located."

'"We can infer the eight keys refer to the eight boys from the land of amrit. The ninth key could be our Rudra. If you notice, the answer to all the puzzles revolve around number twenty-two, and only Rudra's puzzle was different. We identified the answer as the Saturn magic square. Since he seems to be the messenger, his puzzle could be the key for further answers."

'"Now I have a strange feeling we need to establish the relationship between the numbers one to nine in the Saturn magic square and these nine boys."

'Chanakya was listening intently. He nodded, approving Chandragupta's words. "It could be true, Chandragupta. But how can I map the numbers one to nine and the boys? Let me think. I tried to relate these numbers to their dates of birth. But that did not lead us anywhere. What could the link be? Hmm, let me ask the boys. Tell us what your birth star signs are." Guru Chanakya asked.'

'Each one of us told him our star signs.

Name	Bhava	Sarva	Isana	Pasupathi	
Star	Ashwini	Barani	Karthika	Rohini	
Star number	1	2	3	4	
Name	Bhima	Rudra	Ugra	Mahadeva	Shiva
Star	Mirgashirsha	Ardra	Punarvasu	Pushya	Ayilya
Star number	5	6	7	8	9

'Guru Chanakya hit upon an idea. He said, "For ages, the Vedas have been recited and passed on only as a sound. The science of vibrations and frequencies and how they affect people is something that has been around for thousands of years. Divine mantras give energy depending on the sounds and vibrations of the mantras being recited. For example, all galaxies, including ours, are rotating and the sound they make is "OM." That is inaudible to us as the human ear cannot discern sounds of power frequencies. But these cosmic sounds were heard by several Maharishis. Every alphabet pronunciation and vibration can create special results. The maha mantras are letters locked in a mystical way; they will yield results only if they are pronounced properly."

'"Now we have to use these techniques to recite the key clue, "Ramalingaya Namaha." Boys, try to sit in a pattern according to the number assigned to you from one to nine and in the order of the Saturn magic square."

(4) Pasupathi (Rohini star)	(9) Shiva (Ayilya star)	(2) Sarva (Baani star)
(3) Isana (Karthika star)	(5) Bhima (Mrigashirsha star)	(7) Ugra (Punarvasu star)

(8)	(1)	(6)
Mahadeva	Bhava	Rudra
(Pushya star)	(Ashwin star)	(Ardra star)

'Having seated us in the order of the Saturn magic square, Guru Chanakya asked us to wear our twenty-two-faced Rudrakshas, the golden bilva leaves and begin reciting the alphabets of the key clue in the following order.

Pasupathi	Shiva	Sarva
(4) N न	(9) ha ह	(2) Ma म
Isana	Bhima	Ugra
(3) Li लि	(5) Ga गा	(7) Na न
Mahadeva	Bhava	Rudra
(8) Ma म	(1) Ra रा	(6) Ya य

'The sound vibrations took this pattern of the Saturn magic square:

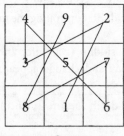

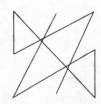

Sound pattern   Sound vibration pattern

'When we recited this pattern, a dramatic thing happened!'

47

'The dried palm leaves flashed messages. As one completed the page, another page's message flashed. There were continuous pages.

'We could tell that each message represented one *shastra* (science). The title of each of the *shastras* flashed first on the dry palm leaf. The eight *shastras* were:

Custodian	Who	Shastra/Science
(1)	Bhava	Karya siddhi (get what you want) and Easarwam (God's status)
(2)	Sarva	Annima siddhi (become small like atom) /Mahima siddhi (growing physical self to incredibly large size).
(3)	Isana	Laghima siddhi (become almost weightless) Garima siddhi (become bulky)
(4)	Pasupathi	Vasithram siddhi (controlling the minds of others) Parakayam siddhi (get into another person's body and change appearences at will)
(5)	Bhima	Death/Anti-death *shastra* (science)
(6)	Rudra	Brahmastra
(7)	Ugra	Memory/Anti-memory *shastra* (science)
(8)	Mahadeva	Gravitational/Anti-gravitational *shastra* (science)

(9)	Shiva	Alchemy *shastra* (science) (creation of philosopher's stone with power to turn base metal sand into gold/silver and vise versa and creation of elixir (amrit) to confer youth/longevity).

'Guru Chanakya was ecstatic. It was the first time I had seen such an expression on his face. "Boys, this is an incredible discovery. Books break the shackles of time. A book is proof that humans are capable of working magic. These are secret shastras. We should not share these secrets with anyone. The biggest Guru mantra is this—never share your secrets with anyone. It will destroy you. The secret has to be kept to the nine of you, me and Chandragupta. These shastras will pave the way for creating Akanda Bharat!"

'"By the way, what about Rudra's palm leaf? Number six, the Ardra star?" Everyone's attention turned to me. Chanakya said that 'Brahmastra' and the 'Gayatri mantra' were written on my leaf: what did that mean?

'Chandragupta said, "Brahmastra is the mother of all missiles—a weapon of mass destruction. It hits the target chosen by the sender and causes total annihilation. In the last Yuga, it was used by chanting this mantra. Does that mean one can release the Brahmastra just by chanting the Gayatri mantra? Can you try, Rudra?"

Brahmastra in Action

'Chanakya intervened, "Unlike normal weapons, it is not held in the hands, nor is it usually kept in a quiver like an ordinary arrow. When the need arises, it is summoned by casting a divine spell. But will that work for just anyone?"

Brahmastra in action

'He continued. "All mantras have great potency. One has to gain siddhi in a particular mantra before it works miracles for him. What is siddhi? Siddhi is nothing but when a *sadhaka* chants with full concentration a particular number of times. Siddhi is nothing but that particular person himself charged with that mighty energy. Rudra can invoke it. Rudra, try to summon the missile with the Gayatri mantra now."

'I tried but had no success. What could we do next? We had all eight *shastras* but the ninth one, the Brahmastra, was eluding us.'

48

'"Brahmastra can be released by chanting the Gayatri mantra in a specific manner, the syllable sounds and pitch may differ from what we normally do during our puja,' Chanakya said. 'The sages of ancient Bharat used to produce various results in the rituals they performed and from the mantras they would recite. The sages learned the mantras with the power of concentration acquired through austerities. See, even the vibrations of *nadis* produce sounds but are not audible to our naked ears unless we make attempts to feel it closely. Science tells us that these are sounds outside the range of human beings in the same way as there is light that does not pass through the lens of the eyes. The sages with their celestial ears could hear the mantras in space; the science of yoga says that if our heart space becomes one with the transcendent outward space, we will be able to listen to the sounds in it. Only those who have attained the state of undifferentiated oneness of all can perceive them. It is in this way that the seers became aware of the mantras and made them known to the world. It must be remembered, they did not create them. They brought us immeasurable blessings by making the mantras from outer space known to us. If the mantras were recited in particular ways, certain amazing results would take place, including changing the weather, producing certain types of living being or even places. Specific mantras could be attached to arrows, with the sound causing powerful explosions when the arrows reach the target."

"'So, a question arises. How do we create the right vibrations while chanting the initiating mantra of the Brahmastra? Let us think. Meanwhile, can you all give the voice commands that you used to initiate these *shastras* while sitting in Saturn magic square positions?"

'When we chanted "Ramalingaya Namaha" sitting in the same order, all the messages on the palm leaves vanished. We realized this was the command that could unlock and lock the accessibility to the *shastras*. What a great discovery! We were all ecstatic. But the Brahmastra was still eluding us.

'We travelled back to Taxila, and stayed in the forest camp set up by Chanakya.

'Chanakya was thinking seriously about how to unlock the Brahmastra's secrets. After considerable deliberations, he said to all of us, "Boys, listen, this is a possible solution. There is one man, Chiranjivi Ashwathama, who was cursed to wander in this Kali Yuga. He knew how to initiate the Brahmastra, even though he did not know how to withdraw it. Only Arjuna can do both, initiate and withdraw the Brahmastra.

"Ashwathama is wandering the forests around Taxila. He joined Alexander's group for a while, but left later. But due to the curse, he lost his memories and knowledge regarding his skills. We need to recreate his memories and revive his skills."

'Mahadeva, one of the eight boys, remarked:

"Guruji, we can use one of the *shastras* of memory which was made available to us."

"'Brilliant idea Mahadeva. We can use that and recreate Ashwathama's memory."

'Chanakya sent his men out to look for Ashwathama.

49

'Ashwathama came to our camp, "The Brahmastra again?" he asked with a big grin on his face.

"'Everyone has to come to me for that. Alexander came to me. But halfway through I walked out of his camp. He promised to destroy King Porus, but he cheated me. He also ditched me, but met with his death at an early age. Now, Chanakya, you are also after me for the Brahmastra?"

"'Alexander's untimely death is not surprising as those who blaspheme against Vedic wisdom, who ridicule the lifestyle recommended in the *shastras* and who deride men of peaceful temperament come to grief very quickly at an early stage of life. But Ashwathama, you are a person imbued with Vedic wisdom. Still you show signs of arrogance."

"Talent is god given; be humble

Fame is man given; be grateful

Conceit is self-given; be careful."

"'We should speak only those words which have the sanction of the *shastras*. And perform those acts which have been carefully considered."

"'Chanakya, you have started your lectures once again. Do that with your students, not me."

"'Let us come to the point, Ashwathama. Please help us with the secret of the Brahmastra. Walk shoulder to shoulder with us in building Akanda Bharat."

"'What Akanda Bharat? You are a poor Brahmin; you have

a young man and nine boys in your gurukul. How can you do it? Don't daydream, Chanakya."

"Ashwathama, you will see us performing that feat soon. But right now, we seek your help in decoding the Brahmastra. We have received word that only the Gayatri mantra can release the weapon. But the command has certain unique sounds and vibration techniques. We request you to teach us to serve a great cause."

"But Chanakya, I have forgotten all of that due to the curse put upon me by Lord Krishna, you know that. And yet you want my support. I am surprised."

"Ashwathama, we have a technique to restore memories. We will perform it on you. Then you can recall the voice command for initiating the Brahmastra."

"Sounds nice, Chanakya. But please note that the Brahmastra will not work in this Kali Yuga where dharma is only twenty-five per cent of that which prevailed in the first four yugas. Dharma has been deteriorating in the ratio of 4:3:2:1 over the past yugas. I doubt whether the voice command will work in Kali Yuga, but let us see."

'Chanakya took him to his chamber and summoned Ugra, the custodian of the memory *shastra*. He did not explain anything to Ashwathama, who was given anaesthesia and lost his senses for a while. Ugra then used the *shastra* and recalled Ashwathama's memories.

'After a few hours, Ashwathama came back to his senses. "I can recall every bit of the Kurukshetra war. You are right, Chanakya. I underestimated you. Give me a grass blade and I can initiate the Brahmastra now."

'He chanted the mantra in a particular peculiar way with different sound vibrations and positioned the grass blade to target the tree, which lay some distance away. The weapon was supposed to target the tree and cause it to burst into flames. This was supposed to check the targeting capability and see if the destruction caused by the Brahmastra could be controlled.

'But to everyone's disappointment, the blade hit the target and fell down. No flames and no damage was caused to the tree.

"I told you, don't waste your time. The Brahmastra will not work in the Kali Yuga. You must do something fruitful, and not waste your time on this."

'Saying this, Ashwathama went away. Again, there was utter frustration in our camp. We were all disappointed, since we had crossed several hurdles, solved puzzles, and worked for this goal. But the whole thing seemed to be a waste. There was gloom all around.

'Guru Chanakya addressed the camp, "Boys, without doing things with full conviction, we call ourselves unlucky and brood over failures. Breaking a cocoon and releasing a butterfly is often detrimental to the butterfly. Nothing worthwhile comes without struggle. Do not be demotivated. Failure is an option, but fear is not."

'Those were great words for the devastated camp. At that hour, the leader of our group, Chandragupta, chipped in with his thoughts.

"If we scrutinize the seal, we can see that we used all the clues, but two things remain unexplained. We did not use the clue "water" and "destroyer guarding" twenty-two jewels. As Guru Chanakya said earlier, this may refer to Rameswaram since the destroyer Lord Shiva is guarding the twenty-two rivers appearing as ponds within his temple there."

"'Let us then move to Rameswaram," Guru Chanakya ordered.'

50

'Rameswaram, located at the very tip of Dakshin Bharat, is gently lapped by the silent waves of the ocean. This conch-shaped island is as ancient as the Ramayana. It is one of the most sacred places of the people of this land.

'Here, there are twenty-two ponds called *theerthams*. The ponds located inside the temple are believed to be from the waters of twenty-two ancient rivers. These twenty-two ponds correspond with the number of arrows in Rama's quiver. Each pond's water has a different taste. It is considered holy to bathe in the waters of these ponds.

'We entered a great temple. We had a darshan of the Ramalinga that evening and returned to our camp for the night.

'A few inscriptions on the temple wall caught the attention of Guru Chanakya. He read them and translated them for us.

"Boys, the ponds in the temple corridor have their own significance. The concept is that just before purifying the soul inside the temple, one can purify the body in these "*theerthams*" or holy ponds. The Setumadhava *theertham* is said to contain the blessings of Goddess Mahalakshmi and to purify the hearts of devotees. The significance of the Kavatcha *theertham* is that one will never go to hell. The Nala *theertham* is meant for getting into heaven. The story behind the Surya *theertham* is that through this, one will get the knowledge of the past, present and future and reach anywhere one wants to in the world. The Ranavimosana *theertham* is meant to get rid of all debts. The Jambava *theertham* offers longevity of life. The Kodi *theertham* is believed to have saved Lord Krishna himself from his sin of killing his Uncle Kamsa. Altogether, there are as many as twenty-two *theerthams*. The Koti *theertham* came into existence when Lord Rama pressed his arrow to the earth at the time of installing the Ramalinga. This water is used for the *abhishek* of the linga today. One can access the sea and the Ramasethu in the sea via this pond."

'Having explained the inscription, Guru Chanakya told us, "Boys, let us bathe in these ponds tomorrow morning. Look for any clues then. Let us retire for now."

'But while everyone else slept, my mind was busy making plans.'

51

'The next morning, all of us got up and went for a bath in these twenty-two ponds. I had planned to swim into the sea and Ramasethu via the last pond, Koti *theertham*. The others did not know my plan. Something in me told me that this adventure of mine might lead me to the last clue that we were looking for. I didn't want the others to doubt me beforehand.

'As all of them completed the bath in the ponds, one of them observed, "Rudra is missing!" There was pandemonium within the group.

'Even Guru Chanakya did not know of my plan. He took them back to the camp and said, "We will wait till tomorrow. Rudra is a gifted boy, born to achieve. He knows how to counter any hurdle."

'I went deep inside the Koti *theertham* pond and ventured into the deep sea after a few hours of swimming. I lost consciousness and did not know what happened.

'Suddenly, I regained consciousness. I looked around and saw I was lying on an elevated part of the ground which looked like a bridge under the sea. I heard a loud voice.

"My dear child, you have come into the territory of Ramasethu. I am Hanuman, and have been guarding this bridge for ages. When everyone left with my Lord Rama to depart for the upper world, I was prepared to stay on earth to recollect every bit of my association with Lord Rama and Mata Sita."

"'This Ramasethu is the bridge constructed by Lord Rama

with the help of vanaras, monkeys to cross over to Lanka and destroy the demon King Ravana. It embodies the memory of Rama Rajya. I will cherish his memory in Ramasethu till the end of this Kali Yuga. I do not allow anyone to enter this area. I am the custodian of Ramasethu. Lord Rama's words resonate with me even today: "Mother and Mother Earth are greater than *swarga*."

"'At the mere sight of Ramasethu, one gets liberation. Ramasethu is worthy of worship by all. It is the flag of Rama's supreme glory.'

"'Why did you come here, my boy? I do not wish to harm you, as you seem to be a blessed one to see me in this Kali Yuga.'

'I was stunned. It was a dream come true.

'I regained my strength and told him the saga of our great hunt.

'Hanuman said to me, "Now I understand why you are here. I know only one person other than Kalki who will come here in this Kali Yuga. You look for clues to the Brahmastra. I will tell you now, but after your lifetime, that secret will stay a secret forever. You have to keep it as a secret as it is protected from mankind to avoid the destruction of humanity."

"'The chants to initiate the Brahmastra will only work till the last Yuga. Now we are in Kali Yuga. Apart from this voice command, you have to apply a mineral over the instrument of the Brahmastra. Which mineral? I know you will ask that."

"You have to apply a reddish mineral* over the Brahmastra

---

*Thorium, a mineral abundant in Ramasethu, is widely held to be the best candidate to solve India's future nuclear needs. This will replace uranium-based nuclear reactors. Thirty per cent of the world's thorium reserves are available in Ramasethu. This is a high energy generating material, as high as the energy of the Brahmastra. Ramasethu is an energy heap created by Lord Rama for future generations.

before launching it with the mantra. That is what will work in this Kali Yuga."

"'You know where this reddish mineral can be found? You see it here. Ramasethu is made of this reddish mineral. The heat flow in Ramasethu is comparable to that of the Himalayan springs. This generates high energy. The sand from this Ramasethu was that used by Mother Sita to create the Ramalinga, which all of us worship in Rameshwar."

"'I am here to protect this region and will not allow the destruction of humanity or the destruction of Ramasethu, the bridge that bears the imprint of Lord Rama's steps. But I will give you a small amount of the mineral enough to make nine astras. You have to protect them from external forces."

"'Now you can go back. I will take you to the Koti *theertham*, the pond through which you came." Thus I reached the temple.

'When I returned to the camp, everyone was thrilled. I narrated this episode to the group.

'We all went back to Taxila after several days of travel.'

52

'Guru Chanakya immediately summoned Ashwathama. We now prepared nine astras with the minerals spread over them.

"This time, Ashwathama, if you initiate any of these astras, it will work as the Brahmastra. But on one condition, you have to teach Rudra the sound, vibration and modulation patterns of the voice command chant to initiate the Brahmastra."

'Ashwathama agreed but he put a counter-condition, saying that if it worked he needed five of the astras as a memory of his enemies, the Pandavas. The condition was agreed upon as there was no other way to make him agree to help us.

'He taught me how to initiate the chant. After that, he chose a tree as a target and launched the astra which had been coated with the mineral powder.

'It worked. The traces of the tree were not visible at all, and total destruction was witnessed by all of us.

'Our camp was jubilant. Ashwathama was given five astras out of nine. One had been used and hence only three were left in our keeping.

'Ashwathama said, "Now my mission is complete. I will die peacefully at the end of this yuga. Every day I will see these five astras, five Pandavas, as my slaves. Thank you, Chanakya, and long live Rudra! You will no longer see me in this region. I am going to the Himalayas for salvation."

'Our camp was jubilant. We had achieved our goal. Now we had to focus on creating Akanda Bharat. Guru Chanakya smiled at us and said, "Success is sweetest only when you have tasted the defeat. Boys, enjoy a break this week. From next week, we start our mission, Akanda Bharat. Chandragupta will be the leader of our army that will be assembled shortly. The nine of you will constitute the "Nava Yuva Sena". Each one of you will be the custodian of the *sastras* in your possession. You will be the commandos who protect Chandragupta and help us cross all the hurdles that come our way."

"'The nine secret *shastras* in our possession should be buried within us. They should not be discussed even with your close relatives or friends, understand?"

'We went out for a short break before we embarked on our mission, Akanda Bharat.'

53

Swastika was curiously listening to the story of the great expedition. 'Commander, this is a thrilling experience! Now you have shared your secrets with me.'

'You came from nowhere and became a part of me, Swastika. You told me all about yourself. Therefore, I didn't feel like keeping anything from you. Even the secret I am supposed to never discuss was shared. Please for heaven's sake keep it secret forever.'

'Commander, did you use those *shastras*? What did you do as part of the mission Akanda Bharat?'

'We spent more than twenty years with Chanakya. All my fellow Yuva Sena soldiers got married and had children, four of them boys and four of them girls. I had been waiting to meet you and get married. See how fate brings people together, Swastika?'

'Oh, the Yuva Sena soldiers are married? Tell me about how you helped Chanakya and Chandragupta build Akanda Bharat.'

'Well, it is a long story lasting twenty years. At many instances, we helped Chandragupta Maurya.

'We were fighting the mighty Magadha kingdom. We did not have their huge army or their massive wealth. We had to adopt guerilla techniques to defeat them.

'That is where our secret *shastras* helped. Dhana Nanda, the mighty Magadha king, kept a huge quantity of gold in an underwater cave in the midst of the Ganga. It was guarded by mighty warriors.

'We used Anima siddhi, became ant-like in size and sneaked into the cave. We used Vasithavam siddhi (controlling the minds of others) to control the minds of the warriors. We made them sleep for a considerable time during our operation. Using alchemy the *shastra*, we turned the massive gold stored inside into liquid mercury and transported it quickly in drums. We replaced the gold heap with a sand heap. When the soldiers woke up, they continued to guard the sand inside the chest, without knowing what it contained.

'Thus we gained the wealth to fight for Akanda Bharat. The looted wealth has to be reused for a good cause, Guru Chanakya used to say.

'Not only that, in the battles we used the death *shastra* to bring back the life of any of our soldiers who had been killed. We controlled the minds of opposing soldiers, confused them and made them fight against their own men. We guarded our Emperor Chandragupta. Even though I am his commander-in-chief, he treats me as his close friend. Since we moved together for so many years and have been shaped by our Guru Chanakya, our friendship runs deep. But I maintain my respect for my emperor, as I cannot deviate from the protocol.

'Guru Chanakya was very particular that we should have the use of the *shastras* at all times. We can access the *shastras* by using the specific voice command; we call it the entry voice command. When this command is used, we have access to the nine sciences. We can also use the same command to exit the access. As a matter of policy, we use the exit commands to close the access only during Navratri and Shivratri.

'Nice Commander, you also give holidays to your secret

shastras,' Swastika joked.

'Well, Swastika, it is time to move to Pataliputra, our capital city. I have received the order from our emperor today. I will take you and your brother with me to my headquarters. I am looking forward to joining my co-commanders soon.'

'Who will be governor here and look after the Massaga fort, Commander?'

'Do not worry; your fort will be taken care of by our Mauryan empire. My brother Mudra has been appointed as governor. My father Devadutta and my mother Ramba Kumari will stay with him. Get ready, tomorrow we are leaving for Pataliputra.'

'Commander, excuse me. I have to pack our bags for a permanent shift to Pataliputra,' Swastika replied and went to pack her things.

PART VI

Samrat Speaks

54

'What are you thinking about so deeply, Samrat? Which part or kingdom do you plan to conquer now? Come back to Taxila, Samrat,' the voice of Helen shook Chandragupta.

'I have been conquering kingdoms easily but now I am captured by the kingdom of love, my queen. Your beauty has conquered me and held me prisoner to love. But we have to move to Pataliputra. There are many ways of binding by which one can be dominated and controlled in this world, but the bond of love is the strongest. Take the case of the humble bee, which although expert at piercing hardened wood, becomes caught in the embrace of its beloved flowers. So, too, am I. But coming back to the realities of life, I have much governance work pending at the Pataliputra palace. We will first have a wedding function along with Rudra, and receive the blessings of Chanakya, our Guru,' Chandragupta said.

'When are we leaving?'

'Tomorrow afternoon. It may take ten days to reach Pataliputra. Rudra is marrying the princess of the Massaga fort. They will be coming from there. Acharya Chanakya is already in Pataliputra making the arrangements for our royal wedding, Helen.'

'But Samrat, I kept my promise. I told you about my past. But you haven't done the same. Let me now hear from you about your past, before I get ready to pack my belongings. When two souls have become one, there should be no secrecy between them, right, Samrat?'

Chandragupta suddenly thought of his Guru Chanakya's words. 'Chandragupta, take this as the most vital Guru mantra. Never share your secrets with anyone, including your wife. Those secrets revealed will come back to hurt you later.' He didn't know why those words came to his mind at that time. But he wanted to reveal all his past to the Greek queen, omitting certain secret details.

'You are right, Helen. I do appreciate the openness between us. Let me share some stories with you.

'Before I go back to my past, let me tell you, Helen, it was love at first sight with you. When I saw you many years ago, playing with your handmaidens, I was smitten by your beauty. Later I became busy with the mission Akanda Bharat. But my wife Durdhara died while giving birth to my son Bindusara. As a widower, I was sad, thinking that I would live the rest of my life alone.

'But when I came to know you live here in Taxila, my first love conquered me again. I confessed my desire to have you as my wife to my Acharya Chanakya. He advised me that the only way was to do battle with your father. The rest is history, Helen.'

'Oh! The real purpose of your war was to conquer me and not Taxila?' Helen countered.

'Perhaps both.'

'Let me hear about your early days, Samrat.' Helen's inquisitiveness continued unabated.

'I brushed our first love aside initially, since I knew you were a Greek princess and there would be no cultural compatibility, and so I married the princess of Magadha, Durdhara.'

55

'Helen, I belong to the Kshatriya clan called "Moriya," which originally ruled Piplivana, a small forest kingdom. My father was murdered by the cruel Magadha king, Dhana Nanda, by deceit and our kingdom was taken over.

'My mother Mura escaped with me and brought me up. She swore revenge against the Magadha king. Along with my mother's milk, I was fed with the desire for revenge against the Magadha king right from my childhood.'

'How and when did you make the acquaintance of your Acharya Chanakya? Who is Chanakya, and where did he come from?' Helen asked.

'Helen, you should address Acharya Chanakya with great respect. He is my Guru, philosopher and guide, and he is not an ordinary person. His mastery of the Vedas is well-known. He seems to have mastered the *Atharva Veda*, yoga, black magic, occult sciences and has a considerable depth of knowledge in our ancient scriptures.

'He was called "Pakshilaswamy" because of his prodigious memory, as he could remember for a *paksha* or fortnight everything he heard once. He was also a master of hundreds of birds, pigeons and hawks, which he employed to carry secret messages.'

'Oh! You were lucky to get such a person as your Guru!' Helen exclaimed.

'Even the king of Taxila respects him for his extraordinary

knowledge. Everyone fears him, and he commands great respect. He is also called the "Black Brahmin" owing to his dark complexion.

'He is very practical in his approach yet he is rooted in spirituality. His self-denial is such that he, the prime minister of the greatest empire of the world, lives in a house which is much poorer than many a humble man's abode. The firm establishment of our ancient dharma is his life's goal and mission. Advice from such a man is priceless.'

'How did you meet him, Samrat?'

'He was insulted by Dhana Nanda in front of learned Brahmins. He made a vow to destroy him. One day he saw me playing with my friends, acting as a king. He saw in me the qualities of a king. Knowing that my family was also looking for vengeance against the king, he took me on as his disciple. He told me to stop being a prisoner of my past. Instead, I had to emerge as an architect of my future. "Take the insults as scars that remind you of your grievances," he said to me. "The worst wounds, the deadliest you face aren't the ones you see outside. They are the ones that bleed internally. Keep those scars as the sparks that convert possibilities into flames of achievements."

'I asked him, "Acharya, can we win against the mighty king?"

'He corrected my thinking with his famous words which always ring in my ears even today. "Unless you perceive your worth, you cannot shine in your life. Perpetual optimism is a force multiplier. Being strong doesn't always mean you can handle what is thrown at you. It just means you are prepared to ignore whatever it is that hurts you. Come out of the grievance of your past. Dream of your future."

'I surrendered myself totally to him saying "Acharya, don't make me your number one, but make me your only one." He shaped me. I am where I am today because of my Acharya.

'I have no idols but I idolize my Acharya for his unceasing determination, dedication and competence. Helen, I become very emotional when I think about Acharya Chanakya.'

'Samrat, I understand your deep bond with your Acharya. Tell me how you won over the Magadha king.'

56

'A good question, Helen, Everyone has asked me this question. How did a poor boy and a Brahmin win a mighty kingdom? For this, you need to know about Dhana Nanda, the unpopular king of the mighty Magadha kingdom.

'Dhana Nanda's great-grandfather had two wives and one of them was the daughter of a barber. So his grandparents, his father and his uncles were often insulted. To take revenge, his grandfather along with his nine sons (including Dhana Nanda's father) made a plan to kill his great-grandfather and the sons of his other wife. After they succeeded, Dhana Nanda's grandfather proclaimed himself king. Later, the throne was given to his father and after that to Dhana Nanda.

'Dhana Nanda was addicted to hoarding treasure. He collected riches to the amount of eighty kotis in a rock in the bed of the Ganga. Levying taxes on the smallest of things, even on animal skins, tree and stones used for houses, he amassed further wealth while causing great harm to the people.

'During Alexander's campaign, King Porus stated the king of Magadha was a man of worthless character and was not held in respect. He was considered the son of a barber. His dynasty was very unpopular among the people and the neighbouring states, and some of the reasons behind this could be their varna, since the Nanda kings were said to be from a low caste.

'With Acharya's guidance and the special skills of our Nava Yuva Sena, I grabbed all the ill-gotten wealth buried in the

Ganga. That wealth would meet the financial needs of the war. Dhana Nanda cried "Alas! We neither enjoyed our stored honey nor gave it to charity and now someone has taken it from us in an instant."

'When some of us questioned the capture of the wealth, Acharya Chanakya's words of wisdom showed us the way. Acharya taught us "Sometimes karma doesn't come around fast enough, and that is why it is essential to plot revenge. We should repay the favours of others with acts of kindness, and so also we must return evil for evil in which there is no sin, for it is necessary to pay a wicked man with his own coin."

'That is how we collected the war chest. Next was the task of building an army. Acharya guided us in this too. "The enemy can be overcome by large numbers, just as grass through its collectiveness wards off erosion caused by heavy rainfall."

'We assembled a huge team comprising mercenaries, frustrated military men from Magadha and also won the support of various kings of Bharat.

'Whenever we felt fear about the opponent's large army, Acharya motivated us by saying, "As soon as fear approaches near, attack and destroy it. We should never show our worry to the opponent. Even if the snake is not poisonous, it should pretend to be venomous. If you stand, you stand, if you sit, you sit, don't wobble. The right attitude with one arm will beat the wrong attitude with two arms every time." We always had a positive outlook, thanks to Acharya.

'Moreover, we worked as a team as Acharya always reminded us. Talents can win only games but teamwork alone can win accomplishments.

'He always projected me as a leader, saying, "Chandragupta, a competent leader can get efficient work from poor troops, while an incapable Dhana Nanda will destroy the best of the troops."

'We adopted five ways of capturing forts in accordance with Acharya's advice—by intrigue, through spies, by winning over the enemies, conquering the cities and their people by siege and by direct assault.

'We fought against Dhana Nanda by using guerilla tactics. After the death of Dhana Nanda, the Nanda empire fell. Our forces besieged Pataliputra. Our troops drew a noose tighter around the city until the Nanda army was defeated. The war brought an end to the Nanda dynasty and established our empire with me as its emperor. We built up a huge army with one crore soldiers, 10,000 elephants, 100,000 horses and 5,000 charioteers.

'Some of the kings who supported us in the war against Magadha asked for a share of the kingdom. Some of them got killed by poison-bearing maidens, some of them through the Acharya's plots.

'My Acharya and my friend Rudra had played a key role in bringing me to my goal. Subsequent to this, we gradually expanded our empire and created Akanda Bharat.'

57

'Apart from your reverence for your Acharya, you also seem to be obsessed with your friend and commander, Rudra. Isn't that so, Samrat?' Helen's questions continued.

'Yes. Why not? He fought all these wars shoulder to shoulder with me; he saved me from complicated situations. Some people go to friends, others go to poetry, some to the wife and some seek other pleasures like alcohol or harems. But I always went to my friends. Lovers have a right to betray you, but friends don't. Friends are like ship lighters on the stormiest nights,' Chandragupta's words were strong.

'Samrat, there is some self-interest in every friendship. There is no friendship without self-interest. This is the bitter truth.'

'Helen, do not suspect my friend, my commander, Rudra, at any time. I would not like an argument against Rudra,' Chandragupta thundered.

Realizing the sensitivity of the issue, Helen changed track. She decided not to talk about Rudra, even though she did not like his closeness to her Samrat.

'Helen, note the words of our Acharya: "Despite growing on the same earth and in the same soil, two plants from the same mother have different characteristics. For man, the way one absorbs the same knowledge from the same teacher and the way one assimilates and utilizes it is what distinguishes one from the other. Chandragupta and Rudra are my distinguished students. They are two different personalities close to my heart. The two will always have to complement each other and never create circumstances of competition with each other."

'Understand, Rudra and I can never be separated, such is our bond. In spite of this privilege, Rudra keeps a respectable distance from me and maintains the protocol.'

'I understand, Samrat. I just asked in order to clarify my own understanding of the people around you. Please do not take it as an insult. By the way, did you ever interact with Alexander at any time?'

58

'"That is a good question, Helen. You want to know whether I met your king, ignoring the advice of Acharya Chanakya. The answer is yes. But the outcome was terrible. I approached him in his darbar at the place of Porus and sought his help in the war against the Magadha king. He refused on the grounds that his troops wanted to go back home. I asked him, "Is it fatigue or fear that drives you back, King Alexander?"

'He grew wild. He told me that he was the lord of Asia and no one should have the courage to ask such questions to him. He ordered his soldiers to arrest me and keep me in a closed chamber. But I escaped.

'That is the only unpleasant encounter I had with your king, Helen. "Failure is an option but fear is not" are the teachings of my Acharya Chanakya. Hence, I had approached him with no fear, unlike the other kings from this land, like Porus or Ambhi. But the result was disastrous. For a while I was dejected that your king had declined to help us against Magadha.

'But Acharya always told me not to seek outside help for dealing with the problems of our land. When I was dejected, Acharya Chanakya pacified me. He said, "Chandragupta, we accept our current competence levels and we refocus around them. Does a rose plant worry about why the lotus flower is not blossoming on its branches? We are what we are. The world does not end with King Alexander's support. Don't worry."

'Later, when we heard about the death of your king under mysterious circumstances, Acharya said, "Who realizes all his happiness or desire? Everything is in the hands of God. We should learn to chase our passion but also to accept the outcome as events unfold."

'Samrat, that is very good advice indeed. What happened after the conquest of Magadha?'

59

'Magadha was won, and our enemies were crushed. We expanded the empire to fulfil our vision of Akanda Bharat. On the coronation day, I recall the oath Acharya asked me to swear—"I take as my guide the hope of a saint—

> On crucial things, unity
> In important things, diversity
> In all things, generosity."

'I follow this maxim in my governance. We had united the whole of northern India under one rule. The Mauryan empire was the first large, powerful, centralized state in Bharat. The *Arthashastra* laid the foundation of the centralized administration of our governance. The empire was divided into administrative districts or zones, each of which had a hierarchy of officials. The topmost officers from these districts or zones reported to me. These officials were responsible for collecting taxes, maintaining the army, completing irrigational projects and maintaining law and order.

'So far, the state has regulated trade, levied taxes and standardized weights and measures. Trade and commerce have also flourished. The state is responsible for providing irrigational facilities, succour, sanitation, and famine relief to the masses. We have implemented a common economic system and enhanced trade and commerce, with increased agricultural productivity under the able guidance of Chanakya.

Hundreds of earlier kingdoms, many small armies, powerful regional chieftains, and internecine warfare, have given way to this disciplined central authority. In the *Arthashastra*, Acharya said, "The king is the supreme head of the state. His duty is mainly ensuring the welfare and happiness of his subjects. He must work eighteen to nineteen hours a day and is to be at the service of his people, courtiers and officers any time of the day." This rule has been followed. The country has prospered during my rule.

'The council of ministers consists of three to twelve members, each being the head of a department. Then there is the state council which could have twelve, sixteen, or twenty members. Besides this, there is the bureaucracy consisting of the Sannidhata (treasury head), Samaharta (chief revenue collector), Purohita (head priest), Senapati (commander of the army), Pratihara (chief of the palace guards), Antarvamisika (head of the harem guards), Durgapala (governor of the fort), Antahala (governor of the frontier), Paur (governor of the capital), Nyayadhisha (chief justice), Prasasta (police chief). Then there are the Tirthas, Amatyas, officers in charge of accounts (controlled by the chief minister Mahamatya): treasury, records, mines, mints, commerce, excise agriculture, toll, public utility and armour.

'The governors or viceroys of provinces are called Mahamatras and if the designation is held by a prince then he is called the Kumara Mahamatra. Assisting them are the Yutas (tax collectors), Rajukas (revenue collectors), Sthanikas and Gopas (district officers). Then there is the local village head called Gramika under whom the village assembly operates.

'The civil courts are called Dharmasthiya and criminal courts are Kantakshodhana.'

'Wow, its all highly organized, Samrat,' exclaimed Helen. 'But my information says you change bedrooms every day to defeat any plots against your life. Your security seems to be extremely strong. Why so highly protected, Samrat? Are there threats against you?'

60

'Since I consolidated the Bharat kingdoms, the crushed kings or their descendants have been trying to kill me through various methods. Hence, Acharya Chanakya made Nava Yuva Sena my first ring of security commandos. Nobody can access me without their scrutiny. Rudra is the chief of this unit. That is why he is always near me.

'A few instances made Acharya deploy this unit to safeguard me. Some of the instances were very serious. But for Rudra's help, I would have been killed long ago.'

'Were there serious threats against your life, Samrat? Can you tell me more about them?' Helen asked.

'There were many such plots against my life.' Chandragupta told the tale.

'One day, I had a slight attack of diarrhoea. The palace physician prepared his well-known medicine for it, and brought it to me in a golden bowl. I suspected nothing at all, and held out my hand for it. But Rudra was there too. It seemed to him that there was a slight and suspicious haziness and discolouration at the sides of the golden bowl. He said to the doctor, "Give it to me before giving it to the king. Why are the sides discoloured?" The doctor's nerves gave way, and his hand trembled as he handed the medicine to Rudra. Rudra poured a little bit into a small dish, and gave it to a parrot which died at once. "You have mixed a deadly poison in this, Doctor," said Rudra to him quietly. "Drink the contents of the bowl at once, or be prepared to be dragged to the gibbet, and hacked to death." The doctor drank the contents without demur, and fell down dead. "Thus perishes one of the greatest doctors of our time," Chanakya said to Rudra. "He was the loyal doctor of the defeated king Dhana Nanda. I had hoped that he had resolved to serve us faithfully. It would not have been prudent to have dismissed or punished him without proof. He was so popular among the people. Of course, I did not want him, even after this traitorous act, to be killed like a common criminal. We respect knowledge and learning. But doctors who try to murder their patients must die. Remove his corpse and hand it over to his relatives for a proper funeral. They cannot complain as he died by drinking his own poison. Well done, Rudra. You caught him at the right time."

'Five days later, Rudra and Acharya saw, on their daily inspection of every room in the palace, a line of ants with particles of food, emerging from a crevice between the wall and the flooring of my bedroom. Nobody took any notice of it except Rudra. His suspicions were roused, because there were no foodstuffs or provisions in the bedroom, so the ants must have got them from some hidden store underneath. Yet none of them knew of any basement there. Rudra tapped the floor gently, and detected a hollow sound indicative of the existence of a tunnel. He asked his co-commandos to watch the precincts, and prevent the escape of hidden assassins by any outlets they might have made. Then Rudra had the floor dug up. Sure enough, there was a tunnel underneath. In it were found Dhana Nanda's loyal men armed with assassins' daggers, and provided with plenty of rice, meat and other edibles to while away their time till the night came. Chanakya had them burnt alive in that very tunnel. Thereafter, he ordered that I sleep in a different bedroom every night. I have eight bedrooms in the palace always ready for occupation. Rudra tells me where I am to sleep every evening.

'A week later, a monkey with a large quantity of inflammable material tied to its tail was made to get on to the roof of the palace after its tail had been ignited. The poor thing jumped from place to place on the roof in its fright, confusion and pain, setting fire to several portions of the building. Fortunately, there was no wind and the fire did not spread. Acharya and I woke up with the alarm being raised by Rudra and the fire was put out quickly. The owner of the monkey, a trusted man of the defeated Magadha king, was found lurking in the palace grounds and was burnt to death then and there. Rudra was asked to keep an eye on monkeys also thereafter.

'A few days later, when I went out to attend a sacrifice, the officiating Brahmin seated me on a cushion near the wall. I heard something hissing. Turning around, I found a full-grown cobra with its hood spread and ready to strike. I sprang forward, and the cobra bit the cushion I had been seated on instead. It was immediately killed. The Brahmin was put into a cage full of poisonous cobras, vipers and scorpions which killed him. Rudra was directed to henceforth examine the king's seating arrangements in advance.

'There were many such attempts made on my life by the trusted officers of the defeated Magadha king. Rudra defeated them all. That is why Rudra personally heads the Nava Yuva Sena, even though he is also the chief of my army.

'Now do you understand why Rudra is important to me, Helen?'

PART VII

Back to Pataliputra

61

The next day, Samrat Chandragupta and Helen, his new queen, were ready to leave. There was one more palanquin carrying nine beautiful Greek girls travelling along with them.

'Who are those beautiful Greek girls? Are they your friends? Are they coming to visit Pataliputra?' Chandragupta asked Helen.

'Samrat, I will introduce them to you.' She then introduced each one to Chandragupta. 'They are Alexia, Diona, Amara, Hera, Aminta, Barbara, Doris, Elissa, Philomena. They are migrating to Pataliputra with me; they will stay with me there. I hope you don't have any objections to this, Samrat?'

'Oh! No, in our land we say "Athithi devo bhava" which means the guest is God. I am quite happy that you are bringing them to our city. You can enjoy the company of your friends. They are most welcome.'

Their journey commenced. Helen gazed at the roads. They were 48 feet wide, had shady trees on both sides with mile stones marking every mile. Wells and ponds dotted them every eight miles. When they crossed the Hydaspes and their chariot passed Bucephalus, Chandragupta pointed out to her the place where Alexander's darbar had been held.

They proceeded to Indraprastha on the Yamuna and then to Hastinapura on the Ganga. They came to Prayag at the confluence of the Ganga and Yamuna. After crossing Benares, they finally reached Pataliputra.

Helen could see evidence of the great fertility of the Ganga. She could also see how well-to-do the people of the city were, their robes worked in gold and ornamented with precious stones. They also wore flowered garments made of finest muslin. There were no slaves in Chandragupta's kingdom.

When they reached it, the city of Pataliputra was rousing itself to its usual hectic and varied activity despite the fast-mounting sun and steadily increasing heat. All its sixty-four gates were open and the 570 towers of the city walls were guarded by sentries on duty. Innumerable bullock carts were coming into the city laden with articles of luxury: corals, pearls, rubies and sapphires from Kerala, diamonds from Kalinga, the finest pearls and cotton fabric from Pandya, silk and wool from Kashmir and Benaras, gold from Sindh, rock salt from the salt range, sandalwood, tiger skins, all kinds of cereals, butter, oil, pepper, ginger, cinnamon.

Thousands were returning in chariots and bullock carts after a bath in the Ganga a few miles to the northeast of the city. On the banks of the river were temples dedicated to Shiva, Indra, Kubera and Vishnu.

The palace had extensive pleasure grounds and gardens abounding in all kinds of flowers, fruit trees and ornamental trees.

Trees of patali or trumpet flowers from which Pataliputra received its name were planted in the grounds. There were several pools inside the palace grounds filled with water from the Ganga.

The palace even though built entirely of wood was of surpassing splendour and magnificence. The royal rooms and audience chamber were luxuriously fitted. Basins and goblets of gold, richly carved tables and chairs made of teak, ebony and rosewood and covered with gold and silver embroidered cloth, copper and brass articles, huge vessels of glazed and ornamental pottery filled with cool water, delicate pieces of ivory casting, and crystal mirrors with polished surfaces decorated these rooms.

Even the ordinary rooms had the appearance of luxury and wealth befitting such a great ruler. The palace occupied a vast square and had four main entrances. Six horsemen and twelve infantrymen stood guard at each of the entrances and were changed every three hours. Men and women were constantly moving in and out of the various gates.

Helen and her friends were completely floored by the beauty and the grandeur of the palace. They retired to their rooms to rest after the journey.

62

The next day, Chandragupta took Queen Helen to the darbar. He introduced her to Acharya Chanakya, Rudra and his council of ministers.

Acharya Chanakya told Samrat Chandragupta that a formal royal wedding had been arranged in the palace for the Samrat and also Rudra and Swastika. The Acharya had made all arrangements, including the distribution of invitations to kings from various kingdoms.

On the second of the Vaishakha month (April) the marriage of Chandragupta and Helen, Rudra and Swastika, was celebrated at Pataliputra with the greatest pomp. Heaps of gold were given to the Brahmins and the poor. Many kings and princes from all over Bharat attended the function. The Kalinga kings, Kirata of Nepal, Kartipura, Benaras, Kashmir, Koshala, Pandya, Chola, Sera kings of the south, were all present.

After the marriage festivities were over and the guests had left, the royal couples quietly retired for their second honeymoon. A few weeks passed in routine life.

Queen Helen was getting used to the new environment and her new life. She spent time with her Greek friends while Samrat was busy with governance.

She spoke to her friends one day. 'Friends, four months have passed since our arrival. Life here is different, but we are getting used to this culture. As a queen I receive tremendous respect from everyone. But still, something is bothering me.'

'What is bothering you, Your Majesty?' Alexia asked her with a smile.

'Oh, no, you have also started addressing me this way! Don't do this to me. We are old friends,' Queen Helen corrected her.

'No, when we are in the Royal Palace, we will continue to give you the respect the queen has to be given. Coming to the issue that is bothering you, please spell it out for us. We are here to help you,' Alexia responded.

'Yes, I am coming to that, Alexia. Here the old man Chanakya and Rudra have the dominant influence on Samrat. The security drills are so tight that every day our king is told which bedroom in the palace he can sleep in. Due to security reasons, they select the room at random and inform the king only two hours before he retires.

'I see this as a serious insult. I do not have right to choose our bedroom. In the name of security, I feel as if I am a royal prisoner.

'Even if I wish to decorate a bedroom with flowers, they are subjected to scrutiny by the so-called Chief Rudra. I am frustrated with the manner in which my privacy is intruded upon. We have to first reduce the dominance of these two—the old man and the so-called great commando Chief Rudra.' The queen was very angry.

Diona intervened. 'Helen, it is not just enough to get angry. We have to act now. If we allow this to continue, we will all be controlled remotely by these two men who have mesmerized our king. The old man's influence in my opinion can never be minimized, as the king owes all his growth to him. But we can try to alienate him from Chief Rudra and his Nava Yuva Sena. We have to be careful in whatever we do. No one should doubt our loyalty to this kingdom.'

'Well said, Diona. I agree with you. Let us first alienate Rudra from the king. Let us attack his skills. Let us create some security breaches. Then I can insist on posting all nine of you as the first ring around us. You are all trained military professionals. I will create a case for posting the first ever female royal commandos as the first layer security around the king. Let us start working towards that immediately,' the queen concluded.

63

A few days later, Chanakya was asking Rudra about a security lapse in the palace.

A great female astrologer recommended by the queen went to the king and spoken to him of many events. After the usual predictions were over, the woman pretended to be a great expert in palmistry too, and requested that she be allowed to see the emperor's hand. When Chandragupta put forth his hand, the astrologer approached near as if to scrutinize the marking on the palm but pulled suddenly out a dagger from her clothes and raised her arm to strike at his chest. Chandragupta caught her arm firmly before the blow could descend, and Rudra ran his sword through the fake astrologer who fell down dead. How had the astrologer been allowed past without being searched was the question. Rudra replied that the lady had come on the queen's recommendation. Since she was a lady, the male commando could not search her.

Rudra was surprised that an acquaintance of the queen's could take such an extreme step. Helen countered Rudra, 'Do you accuse me of being a party to this?' She became very angry.

'Let us not lose our tempers,' Rudra said. 'Let us leave it at this. If any such instance arises in the future, we will explore other ways of strengthening royal security.'

A month later, a party of female horse-dealers from Kashmir came to the emperor, stating that they had a number of fine Aratti, Saindhava, Kambhoja and Vanayu horses, and that he, a connoisseur of horses, might select some. The emperor was surprised. It was the first time he was dealing with women horse-dealers. Finally, accompanied by Chanakya and Rudra, he went to see their horses.

They were indeed excellent animals. But no sooner had Chandragupta begun to examine them, all the horse-dealers took up arms that had been concealed in the stables, and attacked Chandragupta and his men. Chandragupta was an expert horseman; he mounted one of the horses and rode off as directed by Chanakya. Rudra and his Nava Yuva Sena fought with the disappointed horse-dealers, who were afraid of the emperor's counter-attack. They mounted their horses and fled. An investigation was ordered yet again.

64

Rudra was called into Chanakya and Chandragupta's presence. To his surprise, Helen was also in the assembly hall.

'Why did you allow the dealers to gain proximity to Samrat Chandragupta? Did anyone carry out a personal search? Why has this problem arisen again?' Chanakya's voice was sharp.

'No, Acharya, the women showed us a mudhra from Her Majesty, the queen. We did not pursue any security check based on the fact that they were coming from the queen herself,' Rudra replied.

'What? Now the accusation is turning against me. Do you question my loyalty to my husband, Samrat Chandragupta? Mind your words.' Queen Helen was furious.

'Rudra, you are sure you have seen the authenticated mudhra? Were there any witnesses?' Acharya cross-examined him.

'My Nava Yuva Sena witnessed my checking of the mudhra,' Rudra replied.

When his fellow soldiers confirmed it, the queen grew angrier.

'Samrat, I left my people, my country, believing in your love. Here I think horrible charges are being levied against me to frame me in your eyes. All your people are calling me a traitor.' With tears rolling from her eyes, the queen started weeping, and Samrat Chandragupta was embarrassed.

'Helen, please hold on to your emotions. As long as I am

here, no one will dare to charge you. You must rest now. I will join you later. Never ever think that I will abandon you.' Chandragupta consoled her and sent her to her room with an escort.

Once it was just the three of them, he turned to Rudra. 'Rudra, there seems to be a problem between you and the queen. This is happening for the third time. You must never embarrass me. You must lie low and show her the respect due a queen and not argue with her. I cannot speak roughly to her. After all, she gave up everything and chose to come with me. It is you who have to lie low and manage the situation. The security threats are far too many. You are the greatest commando we have. We are proud of you, Rudra. Your achievements are enviable but still, under your command, lapses are occurring. This disturbs me. Please fix it. Do not have an ego clash with the queen. After all, she is my better half. The respect you show me should also to be shown to her.'

'But what I said is true, Samrat. Acharya, you taught me "If you stand, you stand. If you sit, you sit, do not wobble." Hence I struck to the truth. Where did I go wrong?

'I think Her Majesty does not want me here. I do not want to be a bother for you, Samrat. I came to Acharya's camp when I was three. I have spent twenty-five years at your side. And still you do not trust me.'

Acharya intervened. 'Rudra, you are my protégé. I believe you. Something is wrong here. Why should Queen Helen turn against you? Is it because she does not like your proximity to the emperor? Is it because she feels her privacy is being intruded by your security checks? There are more questions than answers. We should not put Chandragupta in embarrassing situations. You must retreat into the background for now. Watch the situation closely and double the security around Chandragupta.

'Do not lose heart. You are the architect of our victory. You have the nine *shastras* under your command and control. Never speak of leaving, Rudra. Also make sure the nine key *shastras* continue to be a guarded secret. I hope you are not closing access to them with your exit command. These are troublesome days. The threat to Chandragupta has not yet waned. Stay vigilant.'

All three agreed to put their heads together and concoct a plan to allay Helen's fears and anger.

65

For a few more weeks, there was no untoward incident within the palace. Everything had settled down, Acharya Chanakya thought.

But to their surprise, another mishap took place.

'Arrest Rudra, the traitor! Arrest Rudra, the traitor!' came the loud shouts of the queen. Acharya Chanakya rushed to the royal bedroom, from where the voices were coming.

Chandragupta, Queen Helen and Rudra were inside the chamber. It was half-past ten, a late hour. At this hour, what was Rudra doing inside the bedroom of the royal couple?

He begged Queen Helen to calm down and asked her, 'What happened?'

'Acharya, you are aware that all the food and drink of the emperor is first tasted by Rudra as a security protocol. Today, I tried to take a sip from a cup of milk he had cleared for the consumption of Samrat Chandragupta.'

'Rudra stopped me. I poured the milk to the cat that was sleeping on the floor. To my shock, the cat died. The milk had poison, but it was cleared for the consumption of Samrat. Had I not intervened, he would have died. Rudra is a killer. Arrest him!' the queen shouted at the top of her voice.

Rudra watched in silence. Samrat Chandragupta was also calm, as though nothing had happened. There were no traces of tension in his body language. The queen was surprised by their behaviour.

Acharya calmed her. 'Helen, listen to me. You have to use the right words. You cannot insult our great warrior, Rudra, like this. You have to understand the situation. Upon my advice, Chandragupta has been given a small dose of poison for the last fifteen years. In order to develop immunity from poisoning by our opponents, he has been prescribed this medicine. Over a period of time, he picked up a great deal of immunity to the poison. No poison can kill him now. The so-called poison maidens operating as royal courtesans in several kingdoms accompany royal guests. In lighter moments, they kill the dignitaries by just kissing them. The royal courtesans take poison every day. We wanted our king to develop immunity against such poison.

'Durdhara, Chandragupta's first wife, took the poisoned milk meant for Chandragupta when she was pregnant. The poison spread inside. It was a question of saving the mother or the son. I ordered surgery immediately and we could save the prince. After the mother died, the poisonous blood stuck to his forehead. He has that mark of a "bindu" now. Hence he is called Bindusara.

'I am telling you this history, Helen, so that you are aware of the past. There is no need for panic. Rudra is not at fault.'

But as the days passed, the war of words continued between Queen Helen and Rudra. Acharya Chanakya told Samrat Chandragupta, 'You have to bring this rivalry to a conclusion. In my opinion, Chandragupta, you have to rouse fear through anger in order to control or confer a favour to protect. But you can never show anger against your lover, the queen. Hence I suggest you show her the favour, the second option to protect her. The security and privacy issues have caused this friction. I suggest you have a group of women commandos as your first layer of protection. Let Rudra's commandos be the second layer. Let the first layer of women commandos be appointed by the queen herself. This may set the friction right.'

'That is a good suggestion, Acharya. I will talk to Helen and close this issue once and for all.' Saying this, Chandragupta went to the queen.

The queen was delighted to hear this. She immediately accepted the suggestion. She said she had nine Greek woman commandos, her very own friends who were well trained in combat. Her plan had succeeded.

All her friends were jubilant on hearing this. They thought that this move would enable them to reduce the dominant influence Rudra held over the Samrat. By pointing the needle of suspicion to Rudra, the queen created doubts in the mind of the emperor and achieved the first step towards the gradual alienation of Rudra.

PART VIII

The Indo-Greek Matrimony

The Indo-Greek Matrimony

66

A new ordinance was promulgamated. 'With immediate effect, the Samrat and her Majesty Queen Helen will be guarded by a new team as the first layer of security. The team will comprise the nine Greek commandos Alexia, Diona, Amara, Hera, Aminta, Barbara, Doris, Elissa, and Philomena. They are well-trained fighters who have adopted the Mauryan empire as their new home. The existing Nava Yuva Sena will become the second layer of royal security.'

This ordinance became the talk of the town. The public started talking about it in their hushed tones.

'Why does our emperor need female guards?'

'Maybe so the queen can be with him and it is, therefore, better to have female guards.'

'But the nine Nava Yuva Sena members are super commandos. They are headed by our great hero, our commander-in-chief, Rudra. They are the architects of the Mauryan empire. They fought great wars and won great victories. Are those female commandos superior to our Nava Yuva Sena? Why are they designated as the first layer of security? Are our heroes not degraded by this appointment? Disgusting! Can we disrespect our greatest warriors just because our emperor loves his new queen? Love is blind, but respectability emanates from the character shown.'

The public sympathy grew in favour of the Nava Yuva Sena.

At this critical hour, the public sentiments were echoed at the meeting of the Nava Yuva Sena, chaired by Acharya Chanakya and Rudra.

67

'Scriptural lessons not put into practice are poison. A meal is poison to him who suffers from indigestion, a social gathering is poison to a poverty-stricken person and a beautiful alien wife is poison to a Kshatriya emperor. She erases his pride.' Pasupathi was the first commando to voice his objection. Some of the others followed.

Ugra's turn

'A wicked wife, a false friend and living in a house with a serpent in it mean nothing but death. Now it is the turn of a wicked wife to cause death.'

Mahadeva

'Untruthfulness, rashness, guile, stupidity, avarice, uncleanliness and cruelty are a woman's seven natural flaws.'

Bhīma

'We have the expertise with which we built the Maurya empire. The entry password ("aindra/ऐन्द्र") and the exit password ("ejat/एजत") to the nine secret shastras were our assets. We can close the access to the nine secret sciences and deny their use to anyone else. Now we are the victims of the royal flaws. Lovers may betray you, but friends never should. The role and importance of a friend is forgotten now.'

Bhava

'With an eye to the public mood, I shall speak that which, when understood, will lead to an understanding of things in their proper perspective. I want to categorically assert here in this hall—"It is better to be without kingdom than to rule over a petty one; better to be without a friend than to befriend a rascal; better to be without a disciple than to have a stupid habit; and better to be without a wife than to have a mad one."'

Rudra

'First of all, you all have to moderate your voices and mind your words. We are sitting before our revered Acharya Chanakya. Words once spit out cannot be taken back. Her Majesty Helen is our queen. If we talk badly of her, we are disrespecting our leader, Samrat Chandragupta. You must recall that he took us as his lifelong friends and companions and created the Nava Yuva Sena when we were unknown. He spoke these words which will always ring in our memories. He said:

"Don't walk behind me, I may not lead. Don't walk in front of me, I may not follow. Just walk beside me and be my friend ever."

'We should always walk shoulder to shoulder with him. The positions are temporary but painstakingly built relationships are permanent. All of you have to cool down. Our Acharya will speak now.'

Acharya looked intensely into each one's eyes. 'Boys, anger vented often hurries towards forgiveness. Anger concealed often hardens into revenge. Therefore, you must show your anger, no problems in that. Don't waste your time on revenge. Those who hurt others will eventually face their own karma.

'Cry, forgive, move on. Let your tears water the seeds of your happiness, not your hatred. Don't have a swollen heart. You can even have a swollen head. You are all great men of high calibre. Great minds have great purposes, others only have wishes. Be a man of purpose.

'I advised Chandragupta to marry Queen Helen. This had two objectives. One, our king, a widower, could marry his first love, and two, we could annex the northwestern frontier to our kingdom from Seleukos without much bloodshed. Our goal was to create Akanda Bharat, where our ancient culture and ethos could thrive without the disturbance of any invasion. The empire would have one ruler, Samrat Chandragupta.

'We are marching towards that. Kingdoms like Kalinga remain to be conquered. Your skill must be directed towards larger goals. Let it not be bogged down by petty issues of who is guarding the king. You are great warriors. You have to look at the larger picture. Let us not lose sight of our grand vision.'

Hearing this, the Nava Yuva Sena soldiers were somewhat consoled, realizing that they had been taken off of routine security tasks to prepare for greater duties.

68

The jubilation in the new commando group did not last long. After six months of work, there was a feeling of frustration among them. They met with their friend and queen, Helen.

'Your Majesty! You got us the job of offering security to you and the Samrat, relegating the Nava Yuva Sena to a secondary level. But we now realize we have become the security guards. We feel cheated!' Diona said.

'What happened?' Helen looked at her.

'Well, the rain which falls upon the sea is useless, so is food for one who is satiated; vain is a gift for one who is wealthy; burning a lamp during the day is useless; giving security jobs to trained commandos is meanness.' Amara was sharp.

'Why do you sound so frustrated? You were drafted into this task with the objective of reducing the dominant influence of Rudra and his men. Instead of achieving that, you are complaining. The domination of the influence of Rudra on our Samrat continues unabated. I am dejected on that count, my friends.'

'The Nava Yuva Sena of Rudra has had the last laugh,' Elissa said. 'After giving us security guard jobs, they continue their secret tasks and assignments. There are lot of activities happening between Acharya, Samrat, Rudra and his men. They meet as a group, don't allow anyone inside, the Samrat interacts with them on any day, and they all have free access to the Samrat without any hindrance. I suspect these men have some special skills and our Samrat relies on them a great deal. They may have pulled away from security matters, but are closely associated with the Samrat on strategy matters. We have to break that bond.'

'How?' asked Queen Helen.

Alexia came up with an idea. 'I think we will have to marry the nine commandos of the Nava Yuva Sena, including Rudra. That is the only way the veil of secrecy can be broken. This is my view.'

'What? Marriage? They are all married men. You cannot lure them to marry you. You are playing with fire,' Queen Helen screamed.

'Why not? We will invite them for a friendly dinner as our colleagues, co-commandos. As we socialize, we get them drunk. Once they are drunk, we will have sexual union with them. They will fall victim to our scheming. Once they rouse themselves, they will realize their mistake. We will complain of rape, and the dharmic Acharya will give a judgement in favour of us, asking them to marry us as second wives.

'Once married, we will use our charm and extract their secrets, if any, which give them that closeness to our Samrat. What do you think?'

'Oh! An atrocious, daring suggestion!' all the others screamed in a chorus.

'The quality of the means is questionable, but the end is realizable. It is a dangerous scheme. If you can make up your minds, I am all right with it,' Queen Helen said. After a long discussion, they agreed to the plan.

69

Amara told her co-commandos, 'Ladies, here is top secret news. Samrat and Queen Helen are going for their second honeymoon to an undisclosed destination for five days. They are planning to try for a baby. Helen does not want to be disturbed for a few days. They also want to be away from any known persons. Even the security is being handled by a new team, giving a few days off to us as well as the Nava Yuva Sena.'

'Then who will look after them?' Diona chipped in.

'Rudra has presented a solution. Some of the top soliders from the Mauryan border security forces have been called in to take over the task of guarding the royal couple. These forces have not even personally seen the Samrat. They have been told to guard the guests who are close to Samrat. Thus, no one will know whom they are guarding. Even the citizens of Pataliputra will not know about the Samrat's trip. Only Chanakya, Rudra and the two commando teams know about it.

'We have been given leave for the next five days. Let us enjoy ourselves, girls,' Amara concluded.

At that time, Hera came up with an idea.

'Hey, we now have the opportunity to execute our plan to bring Rudra and his commandos under our influence. We must invite them to dinner. Now we have holidays, Samrat is away—this is the best time to execute our plan. Are you all with me on this?'

'But how can we make the tough Rudra and his commandos

agree to a banquet with Greek women? It is against their beliefs. I do not think they will agree,' Diona said.

Alexia, the leader of the group, came forward. She said it would be her responsibility to make Rudra and his group agree to spend time with them.

Almost at once, she took up the matter with Rudra. 'Chief, I have a small task for you,' Alexia started.

'For me? What work do you have for me? There seems to be a total lack of connection between your team and mine,' Rudra replied.

'Chief, that is why I want to organize a get together for the team members. We have to break the ice. How long can we keep looking at each other as enemies? Our common enemies are those who plot the downfall of the Mauryan empire. Why don't we spend some time together?'

Rudra's colleagues joined the discussion. An unexpected event took place after that.

70

Alexia invited Rudra and his colleagues to dinner the next day. She explained to them that all her colleagues wanted to interact with them at a personal level.

Ugra, one of Rudra's men asked, 'Fine thought, thanks for the invitation. Shall we bring our wives or is it an invitation for us alone?'

Alexia clarified that it was for the individuals and not the family since if they came with their wives, it would become too formal. The purpose of the dinner was to break the ice between the two teams. Hence, they planned to meet on an informal footing so that in the future, a healthy and easy relationship was established between the two teams.

After a little bit of hesitation, some 'yeses' and some 'nos,' everyone agreed to the dinner.

The next evening, the party commenced at Queen Helen's royal guest house, where the Greek commandos were housed.

The ambience was magical. Young girls and boys were employed to entertain the guests with music and dance. There were ten couches with cushions and low tables. The guests were garlanded by the hosts as they entered the hall, which was decorated with ornamental olive oil lamps. The lighting gave a sober touch and the melodious music created a romantic atmosphere.

The tables in the hall held the best varieties of food—vegetables included asparagus, fennel, cucumbers, chickpeas, celery and the roots of certain edible plants, a host of fruits such as apples, pears, cherries, plums, and varieties of nuts. Olives and olive oil could be seen all over the dishes. Honey was also everywhere on the table. Flat breads and yeasty rolls of different kinds were kept along with olive oil for dipping and black olives for snacking. Varieties of salted fish cooked with olive oil and cumin seeds, neatly stacked pistachios, a bowl of lentils, grapes, various broiled meats flavoured with cumin, figs, dates, almonds drizzled with honey, feta dipped in honey, the list seemed endless.

Wines flavoured with pine resin, wine mixed with perfume, cooked wine, sweet wine, herbal wine and grappa were kept ready for serving.

Rudra and his colleagues were astonished by the great hospitality. They had not expected such a wonderful welcome from the women they still saw as their rivals in some way.

71

Before coming to the party, Rudra had a quick chat with his colleagues.

'Friends, we need to keep an open mind and try to use this opportunity to come closer to the other team. But on no occasion we should talk about the secret sciences in our custody. Moreover, please note that all the concerned custodians can at any time initiate their sciences for the protection of the empire. They are all open to their access, since we have initiated them with our entry commands. We have never closed access. We use the exit voice commands only during Navratri and Shivratri. Be careful about maintaining the veil of secrecy over the nine sciences which are hidden from the public eye.'

Everyone was reminded of their responsibilities before the party. The party hall had only the nine 'Nava Yuva Sena' and the nine women commandos.

Alexia welcomed each one with a rose garland. Everyone was seated. Amara opened the conversation while the others served them wines, fruits, nuts and breads.

'We have a tradition of playing some games so that the guests can shed their inhibitions. Now we want to know more about each other. That is the objective of this party.

'If we do that through a game, our inhibitions will leave us and our involvement will be greater. Therefore, I am pleased to introduce this game to all of you—"Complementing Pair." Each of the girls will draw a slip from this jar, which has the names of our guests. The man who bears the name on the drawn slip will be her partner. Both will spend an hour together in a separate room. They will learn of each other's past experiences, tastes, preferences, likes and dislikes. All nine pairs will do the same in separate rooms. Once the understanding phase of the pair is over, a member of each pair will be asked questions about the other. Whichever pair gives the best answers will be crowned as the "Best Complementing Pair". This game will enable us to know more about each other well in an informal and playful manner. Are you all ready, friends?'

The lots were drawn and the following pairs resulted.

Rudra and Alexia
Bhava and Diona
Sarva and Amara
Isana and Hera
Pasupathi and Aminta
Bhima and Barbara
Ugra and Doris
Mahadeva and Elissa
Shiva and Philomena

Each of the pairs went to separate rooms to learn about each other, in accordance with the rules of the game.

72

The Greek commandos played a trick on each of the Nava Yuva Sena soldiers. They exchanged glances, established direct eye contact with them. Each one of them stared at their partner when their eyes met theirs. They stared into their eyes for a second or two and then looked away quickly before it became awkward.

They repeated these actions to make clear their intentions, and thus the game of seduction commenced. The eye contact, the seductive words were put to use by the Greek ladies. They used words in many forms—filled with spice, passion, desire, sensuality. It was seduction at its best. They went close to their partners' ears, offered them the finest of the wine in their husky voices.

The men took their wine glasses, gulped the contents in one shot and asked for more. They did not know that intoxicating elements had been mixed in the wine. They were slowly losing their senses and throwing their self-control to the winds. They started blabbering at their partners, and the women pretended to be attentive to their conversations.

Their lips touched their partner's brain as they touched their lips, as though they were vehicles of some vague speech; they felt an unknown and timid pressure darker than the swoon of sin, safer than sound or odour.

In short, the men were under the control of the women, tight in their embrace.

With words, body language, eye contact, the men were totally seduced by the Greek commandos. They started uttering seductive words into the ears of their ladies, moving closer to them.

The atmosphere turned into a lover's paradise. Each pair became two bodies in one soul. Instead of learning about each other's past, they were consumed by the need to know each other physically. The sexual union between each pair was complete. The female commandos had achieved what they wanted.

The problems began the next day.

73

The next morning there came a frantic call from the chief police officer or Prasasta to Acharya Chanakya.

'Acharya, nine Greek lady commandos ask me to file their rape complaints against the nine Nava Yuva Sena commandos, including Rudra. What should I do, Acharya?'

'Do not take the written complaint from the Greek commandos. Ask them to meet me.'

Acharya Chanakya quickly acted on his own initiative. He did not want the news to spread to the public, especially since the Samrat was away.

He summoned all the men and women commandos to his office. Before he could start speaking, Alexia began to cry.

'Acharya. We were raped by the Nava Yuva Sena. We left our country based on the hope and promises that your kingdom offered. Now we are shattered. Our lives have been ruined. We want justice.'

'What happened? The Nava Yuva Sena are men of character and competence. Tell me what happened. Stop crying.'

Amara explained what had happened right from the reason for the party, and how the party turned into a rapist's paradise.

Acharya did not look at Rudra. He looked at the others. 'What is your explanation, boys? I brought you up. I infused character and competence in you in your early days. Is this the reward you are giving me? It is disgusting to hear about such an episode in the palace. Explain yourselves.'

Ugra said, 'Acharya, we were trapped.'

'The Greek women, for whatever reason, wanted to trap us. They seduced us. It was a seduction by these ladies and not rape.'

'Seduction is fanning the desire of someone. But in your case it seems you have been enticed into doing what you all secretly wanted already. You apparently did not require a lot of fanning of desires. You are also responsible. You went to the party with that thought. Is that not so?'

Mahadeva said:

'Acharya, please allow us to defend ourselves. A woman may forgive the man who tries to seduce her, but a man never misses an opportunity when it is offered. We were in the second situation. It was not a deliberate attempt to rape on our part. We were forced into drinking and intoxicated with wine, we lost our senses and control, and the result is this episode.'

Acharya looked at the women.

'The line between seduction and solicitation is very blurred, and deep down everyone knows it. Is it seduction or rape? Who seduced whom?'

The women began weeping. 'Acharya, we fear we will not get the justice in this court, as these men were brought up by you. We pray that this session be adjourned and re-assembled when the Samrat and our Queen Helen take the chair.'

Acharya Chanakya did not want them to fear that justice would be denied to them. Hence he agreed for one-week adjournment till the Samrat had arrived with the condition that no one should talk about the episode to anyone outside, as the prestige of the palace was involved. He adjourned the court.

However, the women were wondering why he had spared Rudra. Was it because of his extraordinary attachment to him? They decided to complain about this to their queen.

74

The Samrat and Queen Helen came back to Pataliputra the next week. They were briefed on what had happened. The Samrat was very angry. He was surprised that men of high calibre like Rudra had been involved in such a dirty incident.

The court reassembled with the Samrat and Queen Helen on the chair.

Acharya Chanakya narrated the incident and spoke of the last hearing. Having completed his cross-examination in the past week, Acharya Chanakya summarized his submissions.

'Samrat Chandragupta, men will usually not overlook any erotic opportunity. A man's first glance probes every sensuality, and he explores it without discriminating between his friend's wife and the prostitute who opens the door to him. But men of character are exceptions to this. Their self-control cannot be shaken under any circumstances. In this case, I cannot put that tag of "men of unshakable character" to any one of the Sena. The women here receive the benefit of doubt.

'The question is who is telling the truth. Was it the men or the women? Each one is pointing fingers at the others. In a kingdom, a drunken king was once killed by his female aide de camp for getting drunk and making improper proposals to her, and thereby disgracing his throne and country. The next king not only did not punish her but married her, seeing the sound principles she held. This is our *parampara*. We come from the illustrious culture that worships females as goddesses and the utmost respect is given to them in our daily life.

'Here the benefit of doubt is in favour of the females.

'The dissatisfaction of the emperor regarding his territory expansion and the satisfaction of the Brahmin regarding his material possessions can be taken for granted. The same way, the consent of the paid prostitute and the dissent of a virgin to a sexual union with a stranger are to be taken for granted. Hence the lady unmarried virgin commandos of reputed families get the benefit of doubt—their dissent for sex can be taken for granted.'

'But Acharya,' Rudra said, 'the Nava Yuva Sena are not saints, nor the Greek ladies devout housewives. Either of them can cross limits, hence the benefit of doubt exists on both sides.'

Before Rudra could conclude, Queen Helen shouted, 'Stop it, Rudra! You are one of the accused. Please keep quiet.'

Samrat Chandragupta calmed her and went on to pronounce the judgement.

'We have a strict law that even while marching into an enemy's kingdom, our soldiers should not harm or rape any civilians. Stemming from our strict laws against rape, I pronounce the judgement today. The unmarried women who lost their virginity must be given restitution. The deed is more heinous as it has been done to our guests who have adopted our land, reposing full faith in us. Therefore, in this case I grant the priviledge of deciding the quantum of punishment to the lady commandos. Ladies, you may come forward and let the emperor know your wishes. We will confirm it as the final judgement of the emperor.'

Hearing this, the lady commandos went into a huddle and after some time, Philomena stood before the emperor and said, 'We never asked for such unfortunate circumstances to have come to pass. We have two paths in front of us now, one of hate and one of love. We have received a lot of love and support from this land, and so we will adopt the path of love. We ask that we be married to the Sena commandos and given the same status as their current wives. The Sena are also brave men who have had an exemplary record till date. We do not want this stigma and guilt to be part of their lives. The kingdom should not lose any more security. We ask that the commados continue to respect us and treat us with love, compassion and care and we will surely reciprocate the same. We want to get this incident to be in the past and seek to convert this adversity into an opportunity to better all of our lives.'

'Therefore, the following pairs have to get married, even if it is a second marriage for the seducer,' said the emperor.

'Bhava and Diona
Sarva and Amara
Isana and Hera
Pasupathi and Aminta
Bhima and Barbara
Ugra and Doris
Mahadeva and Elissa
Shiva and Philomena
Visaka and Alexia'

'What? The last one is the mistake. It has to be Rudra and Alexia,' screamed Queen Helen. All the ladies were startled.

Alexia cried, 'How can I marry someone other than the seducer? Who is this man, Visaka? Why has the court given a judgement favouring Rudra? All the Yuva Sena should be equal in the eyes of the law. Why is there special treatment given to him?'

Helen joined Alexia in her protest.

When summoned, it turned out that Visaka was none other than the one-eyed prince, the brother-in-law of Rudra.

Rudra explained it. When everyone was busy with their partners, Alexia and Rudra had been left alone. But when Alexia offered him the laced wine, Rudra forced her to drink it herself. Alexia got drunk, and began losing her senses.

At that time Visaka had come with a message from Acharya. He had been called away, and left Visaka in his place. Having lost her senses, Alexia did not make out that Visaka was standing in for Rudra.

Visaka had been seduced by Alexia.

75

Even as they retired to their rooms, Helen did not give up her argument against Rudra. 'Samrat, I never thought you and your Acharya Chanakya would stoop to this level of creating a drama to save Rudra. This is unfair, Samrat.'

'Helen, why do you suspect us? We never deviate from justice. We explained to you that Rudra was not there at all. He was drafted on an emergency assignment.'

'Tell me, Samrat, what emergency assignment arose in the absence of the Mauryan emperor in Pataliputra?'

'Helen, we did not want to reveal the full details of this confidential assignment. This cannot be disclosed to the outside world. This news is being held back from the public due to the sensitivity of the matter.'

'Samrat, I still have a feeling that you are shielding Rudra from justice.'

'Helen, why should I hide the truth from you? I will tell you the details of the assignment, but you must keep it to yourself.'

'Bindusara went out with his friends to the bordering state of Kalinga. Kalinga was once ruled by the previous Magadha emperor. But in the tussle for the throne, the state exerted force and won its independence. Even though under my rule the empire has expanded across the land, Kalinga remains outside of our control.

'The soldiers of this kingdom adopt guerrilla tactics and

wage proxy wars against us. When Bindusara was on a visit to the border areas of Kalinga, he was foxed by the Chief Commander Anandasayana and was taken captive. He was kept in their Ganga Palace in the middle of the Ganga.

'Messengers were sent to Pataliputra by Anandasayana, stating that he would kill Bindusara if his demands were not met. He wanted a letter bearing the royal mudhra, ceding our territory and accepting their control over us.

'We were gone from the palace. Acharya Chanakya had to handle the situation on his own, and could not reach us for consultation.

'Acharya did not want to lose time. He did not want the public to know anything about this. He had to solve the problem quickly. He had only one option: to pull Rudra out of the party.

'He sent an urgent message through Visaka. You know what happened after Rudra left the party.'

'Rudra reached Acharya Chanakya's office, and Acharya's first question was, "Rudra, are your secret sciences accessible?"

'Rudra said, "Acharya, the secret *shastras* are accessible."

'Then Acharya explained the situation. He gave him a letter accepting the demands of the Kalinga commander, affixed the royal seal and asked Rudra to deliver it to Anandasayana and bring back the prince. Rudra knew what Acharya wanted him to do.

'Rudra reached the Ganga Palace, delivered the letter, and brought back the Crown Prince. On his way back, he used the astra and completely destroyed the palace. The palace sank into the Ganga. There are now no traces of it. All the men inside died.

'The commander was also killed in the process. Without

anyone being the wiser, Rudra brought the prince back to the city. It was business as usual.'

'That is highly interesting, Samrat. What are the secret *shastras*? What is this special astra?' Helen was inquisitive.

Samrat did not want to elaborate. He did not want to give the details of the Brahmastra to her, as he had been warned not to divulge them to anyone.

But Queen Helen had now learned that secret *shastras* were known to the Nava Yuva Sena. She knew that she and her friends had made the right move. The marriages would enable them to learn more about the secret *shastras*.

Soon, all the eight Nava Yuva Sena and eight of the lady commandos were married in accordance with the judgement. Alexia was married to Visaka, Rudra's brother-in-law.

The weddings were the talk of the city.

PART IX

The Tragedy Struck

76

After the marriage ceremonies took place , the lady commandos moved into the houses of the Nava Yuva Sena. Each lived in the same house as the first wife. Each of these men had a child from the first wife—four of them had sons and the other four had daughters.

All of them lived happily. There was perfect harmony between the wives of each of these men. To their credit, the Greek wives adjusted well to their new homes and loved their husbands very much.

Even the men were surprised at this and they became very close to their Greek wives. Harmony prevailed.

But on one count, the differences were widened. Helen and Rudra were still not on good terms. Helen was still angry that Rudra had escaped the trap.

When Helen met her friends, they told her that through their husbands, they had learned of some special sciences, and that Rudra was the grand keeper of these secrets. They were unable to learn anymore details, except that the sciences were being guarded for security reasons; if they fell into the wrong hands, utter destruction would ensue.

To Helen, it seemed that Rudra's importance, far from decreasing, was growing every day.

But the women could provide her assistance in one thing. They could create a rift between Rudra and the Nava Yuva Sena. They had brainwashed their husbands, telling them that the secret sciences had to be made public so that enemies would learn that the Mauryan empire was in possession of them, and hence become fearful. Furthermore, if the *shastras* weren't taught to other people, future generations would lose out.

Four of the Nava Yuva Sena commandos raised this issue with Rudra, who cut them off at once. He said that the sciences had been hidden from humanity to avoid the destruction of mankind. They were known to them due to the Chiranjivis, and they had promised to keep the *shastras* a secret.

This difference of opinion slowly created a schism among the Nava Yuva Sena, but Acharya still attempted to hold them together. Nonetheless, Helen was confident that one day the differences would result in a battle. She was waiting for that day.

Meanwhile, she gave birth to a prince. He was named Uranus Gupta. On the same day, Crown Prince Bindusara's wife gave birth to a second son, Ashoka.

The happy occasion was celebrated across the empire. During this phase, all the Greek women gave birth to children as well. Four of them had daughters and the other four had sons. Thus four of the Nava Yuva Sena had one son with the first wife and one daughter with the Greek wife. The other four had one daughter with the first wife and one son with the Greek wife.

There was a baby boom in the palace, and the happiness spread all over Pataliputra and beyond. The only people who had not been blessed with children were Rudra and Swastika. But this issue did not in any way affect their love or affection for one another.

The security of the Samrat seemed assured, and there were no lapses on that front. The Nava Yuva Sena focused their efforts on building the Mauryan army and expanding the empire.

The differences between the Nava Yuva Sena commandos were increasing as time went by. The issue of the *shastras* had become quite a point of discord.

As the children of his colleagues grew up, Rudra took responsibility for shaping them into a new Nava Yuva Sena, continuing the tradition established by Chanakya.

Out of all the children, Uranus Gupta, the Indo-Greek prince and Ashoka turned out to be closest to Rudra. The three were almost inseparable.

Queen Helen did not like the fact that her son was so close to Rudra, but she could do nothing about it.

Samrat Chandragupta once remarked to Acharya, 'Bindusara can be a king of a small kingdom but I do not see him as an emperor. I see all the qualities of an emperor in my grandson Ashoka, even though he is the youngest. I am happy Rudra is shaping Ashoka and Uranus Gupta. I see Ashoka as taking over my role, and Uranus Gupta as chief commander to Ashoka, playing Rudra's role in the years ahead.'

Acharya Chanakya acknowledged the Samrat's grand vision. Life seemed to be moving peacefully, until a tragedy shook the palace.

Rudra and his men went to Benaras to conduct the annual Mauryan military sports event. Many members of the army came to take part.

While the event was in progress, tragedy struck. Four of the Nava Yuva Sena colleagues of Rudra—Ugra, Bhava, Bhima and Mahadev—were hit by something and fell dead.

They lay in a pool of blood. Rudra came to their aid, but nothing could save them. What caused their death, which object hit them—no clues were available. This happened in broad daylight in front of everyone.

The news spread like wild fire. Rudra and the remaining Nava Yuva Sena took the bodies and rushed to Pataliputra. After an initial postmortem, the bodies were cremated.

The wives of the men complained against Rudra. They said that Rudra had killed their husbands due to the differences of opinion they had over the last few years. Rudra tried to stop them, but the women could not be persuaded otherwise.

The postmortem report declared that the deaths had not been natural. The men had been struck by a sharp object that killed them. Upon receiving the report, Queen Helen insisted that Rudra be arrested. Neither Samrat nor Acharya Chanakya could stop such a move since the evidence seemed to go against Rudra. The men had been standing next to Rudra at the time of their death.

Rudra was jailed and put in an isolated cell.

The next morning, visitors were allowed. Swastika, his brother-in-law Visaka and the remaining Nava Yuva Sena came to see him. They asked him one question—'Did you do this, Rudra?' But his 'No' did not seem to convince anyone.

'It is better to live under a tree in a jungle inhabited by tigers and elephants than to live as a convict amongst criminals,' Rudra thought. 'But, what can I do? Fate has driven me here.'

That first afternoon, Acharya Chanakya came to visit him. 'Rudra, I know this is not your fault. I know my favourite student. Some foul play has happened. We will find out what it was, do not worry. This is a passing phase.

'I always told you that we should deal cautiously with fire, water, women, foolish people, serpents and members of the royal family, for they may be fatal. I don't know who this is—is it Queen Helen or your own colleagues? Whom do you suspect?'

'I do not know. Some time ago, a sharp difference of opinion erupted in the group. The men who were killed wanted to speak out about our secret sciences. I refused. Overruling my orders, they taught the entry and exit commands to their sons. Now even though they are no more, at least there will be continuity in accessing these secret sciences.

'I do not know whom to suspect. I have doubts about Queen Helen. I have long suspected her of trying to steal the *shastras* for the Greeks. Perhaps what Alexander and Seleukos could not do with the strength of their weapons, she wanted to do with false love. But I have no evidence. These are suspicions that I cannot discuss with our king. He will think I am creating a gulf between him and his wife. Therefore, I prefer to stay silent without defending myself. What option do I have, Acharya?'

79

Acharya did not want to leave the matter at that stage. He asked Rudra whether the accesses to the secret *shastras* were available at that hour. He confirmed that exit voice commands had not been used to close off access before the death of the four commandos.

Upon confirmation, he immediately called for Pasupathi, who was the custodian of the secret 'Vasithram siddhi' (controlling the minds of others) and 'Parakayam siddhi' (to get into other bodies).

Acharya instructed Pasupathi to get into the body of Rudra and enable him to get into his, while controlling the minds of all the prisoners and guards around. Acharya instructed Rudra to take at most three months to complete his mission. 'I do not know what you will investigate. But come back with evidence. For three months I will manage Pasupathi's family—I will tell Pasupathi's family that I have sent him on a special assignment to border areas. But I cannot handle more than three months. Rudra, are you listening?'

Rudra agreed without knowing what his plans would be. He wanted to first come out and think.

The first stage was completed, and Rudra moved into Pasupathi's body. He left with Acharya Chanakya, and no one seemed to suspect a thing.

Where to go next? Acharya Chanakya took him to his house and they began to hatch a plan.

Meanwhile, Queen Helen continued to rail against Rudra. She was blaming the Samrat for reposing too much faith in him. She thought that was the right time to alienate him from the Samrat.

For his part, the Samrat was helpless. He did not react to Helen's jibes, wondering how Rudra's fate would unfold. His absence would also weaken the Mauryan army.

PART X

The Unresolved Puzzle

80

'I am angry with the developments. I am angry with myself. Why did I travel with the commandos who were killed in my presence? I am angry with my own fate, Acharya,' Rudra burst out.

'Not accepting situtions that lie beyond our control leads to anger. Accept that your travelling with them was your karma. Once you accept it, you will be able to tolerate the consequences, Rudra,' Acharya said softly.

'Rudra, when a diamond is polished, it will experience pain. But at the end of it, it will glitter. Go through pain calmly, live with hope.

'Winning is easy, don't panic. People around you first ignore you, then mock you, then fight you and you win. You may cross all hurdles, but finally, Rudra, you will win.

'Rudra, let us look ahead. There is no point in worrying. You must revisit the scene of the crime. Try to think calmly. You may find results. The weapon used for the crime has not been traced yet. Could it be a mythical weapon? Who can use them in this Kali Yuga?'

At that point, a thought flashed in Rudra's mind. 'Yes, Acharya. I will go to the scene and release one Brahmastra, targeting the culprit responsible for the crime.'

Saying this, he left for Benaras. He did not want to target the culprit directly; instead, he wanted to find him alive. He took the remaining three members of the Nava Yuva Sena

.

..dra invoked the Brahmastra, targeting the place where
culprit was located. He followed the direction of the
.rahmastra along with the three soldiers.

The astra went north of Pataliputra and landed in the
forest located on the outskirts of the city. Rudra went into
the forest and saw a group of twenty-five people.

81

As they neared the group, Rudra was shocked by what he saw. It was none other than Ashwathama, talking to the group. Rudra was not able to see who they were, as he was staring at them from a distance. But he could hear their voices.

'We have killed four of Rudra's men with four out of the five Brahmastras. I genuinely believed that I would retire to the foothills of the Himalayas, but the treacherous Maurya married a Greek woman who belongs to the race of that cheating Alexander. This angered me. Since I had been in the Himalayas, I was not aware of all these developments till you came and told me.

'I have reserved one last Brahmastra to target Chandragupta. But I have not decided on the timing yet. I was surprised that you stood against him, given your own son is the rising star in Maurya camp. What provoked you?' Ashwathama asked the men opposite to him.

Rudra looked at them closely. There stood Devadutta, his father, and Mudra, his brother. What were they doing here? 'I made Mudra the governor of the Massaga fort and asked him to take care of my father. How could they turn against Samrat Chandragupta?' Rudra wondered.

He asked his colleagues to stay away for a while, asked them to rest in the shade of a far-off tree. Then he walked alone, assuming his real form, into the camp.

When they saw Rudra, all of the men around Ashwathama

were stunned. Rudra looked around. About twenty men were making astras.

'What a surprise, Rudra! How did you find us? We have set up a missile factory in this forest. We will make more Brahmastras targeting your emperor and his men. Thank you for bringing back my memory. I retired to the forests out of saintly motives, but your father pulled me back into the world of vengeance.'

Rudra looked at his father, 'Pithaji, you too, are in this dirty game? I gave a governor's position to my brother. How can you go against the Samrat? What happened now?'

'Rudra, note one thing. There will be a threat to your life when you reach the age of thirty, according to your horoscope. I thought you were waiting to seize the right opportunity to become emperor some day. Instead, you became a pet dog, dancing to the tune of your master. You may reach your end soon. When will my dream of seeing my lineage on the throne be fulfilled? I have been serving kings all my life. Now I want to sit in the palanquins along with my sons. Is that wrong? You don't have children. If not you, I want to see your brother on the throne. I can no longer expect this from you, as you became so devoted to your Samrat, never visited or cared for us for the last five years. Then I thought of seeking someone with the great astra, who can take on the mighty Samrat Chandragupta. I met Ashwathama at the foothills of Himalayas. He planned this attempt on your Samrat.' Rudra's father Devadutta explained the plan.

Rudra knew that he had to handle this tactfully, as there was one more Brahmastra targeted on his king. He needed to speak their language in order to save his Samrat. He knew what he had to do.

82

'Pithaji, I understand you. Your ambition is to see your lineage reach the emperor's status. Don't you think I am with you on this? However, you cannot dethrone a mighty emperor overnight. The military is with him, the council of ministers is with him. I have to establish my credibility with all these stakeholders before I launch a coup against my emperor. That is why I am building up my stature in the palace.

'Since I am the only one apart from Ashwathama who can launch the Brahmastra, where is the question of my becoming a pet dog with a wagging tail? Pithaji, we will unseat the Samrat. Now the time has come, and I do not want to delay anymore.'

Devadutta could not believe his ears.

Rudra looked at Ashwathama. 'Ashwathama, you are making these missiles here. You have also got your memory back. But don't you know that the Brahmastra in this Kali Yuga needs not only the voice command but also that red minerals need to be applied?'

'You are right, Rudra. Where can we find these minerals?' Ashwathama was restless.

'I brought them from from Ramasethu, the bridge Lord Rama constructed between Rameswaram and Lanka. I will take you there. We will collect enough to make more Brahmastras. Let us leave now.

'But before that, I have one request. Let me take on the form of Pasupathi, as I will be travelling with some of my colleagues. But they do not need to know our true purposes. We need to do this so that the operation will remain a secret till we accomplish our goal. Otherwise the spies of Chanakya will track us.'

Rudra moved, donned his false identity, took his co-commandos and travelled with Ashwathama to Rameswaram. He asked his father to stay with his brother in the forest camp till he returned.

83

When they reached Rameswaram, Rudra took only Ashwathama to the temple. Before that, he asked his colleagues to use the anti-memory *shastra* to erase Ashwathama's memory. He told his colleagues that he was the one who had killed their fellows. Together, they erased Ashwathama's memory of the initiating and exiting voice commands for the Brahmastra.

Rudra then took him to the Kodi *theertham*, the last pond in the temple. He took a dip in the pond with Ashwathama, took him deep into it till they reached the Ramasethu.

He showed Ashwathama the huge cache of red minerals. Ashwathama was astonished. 'The store is huge! With this quantity we can conquer the whole world.' Ashwathama could not control his excitement. He also did not realize that his memory containing the initiating voice command mantras had already been erased.

Rudra created an entrance under the Ramasethu bridge and took Ashwathama into the underground tunnel.

Once he was inside, Rudra closed the tunnel with Ashwathama inside. He came out and swam back to the temple. Ashwathama would stay inside the tunnel forever. Escape would be impossible.

With the mission complete, he took his colleagues back to the forest. He asked his father to accompany him, along with his brother. He told them that Ashwathama had already gone to Pataliputra to finish the Samrat.

Believing Rudra, his father and brother followed him. Before reaching the palace, Rudra sent word to Acharya through his colleagues, requesting him to arrange an emergency meeting with the Samrat.

Rudra reached the palace. He met Acharya and Samrat Chandragupta and told them about the whole episode.

Having completed his sting operation, he took on his true form as Rudra and asked the Samrat to punish his father and brother for their treason. Acharya Chanakya was shocked that Rudra's father had tried to kill the king. He looked at Devadutta, and said, 'Devadutta, the happiest people don't necessarily have the best of everything, they just make the best of everything they have. I never aspired to be a king, and I am happy to be his Guru. I never thought you would aspire to be something you are not. Excessive greed has driven you mad.'

Rudra's father and brother were put in prison. Samrat was proud of Rudra. He embraced Rudra and said, 'The sun may rise in the west instead of the east, but my Rudra will never waver in his loyalty to me.'

Queen Helen learned about the extraordinary powers of Rudra, his team's access to the special sciences, including Brahmastra and amrit, and above all, his unwavering loyalty to the Mauryan empire.

Helen spoke thus to him: 'Rudra, please forgive me for the strong words I used against you. Now we all know your true character. We are proud to have you with us.'

The queen's words moved Rudra. He was very happy that everything had ended well.

PART XI

The Mysterious Murder

84

300 BC

Rudra began teaching the secrets of the Brahmastra to Uranus Gupta, whom he saw as the future commander-in-chief for Ashoka.

Queen Helen was happy that her son was being taught by Rudra. The friction in their relationships had ceased to exist now, and life in the palace was overwhelmingly peaceful.

The fortieth birthday of Samrat Chandragupta was celebrated in the Karthiga month. Great celebrations were organized across the kingdom. During the same time, Rudra too neared completion of thirty years. Swastika was worried about his horoscope, and the predictions it had given him. She urged him constantly to be careful.

On a Friday, Sukara vara, a grand puja, was organized in the Vishnu temple. After it was over, all the royal guests left.

Rudra had arrived with Uranus Gupta and Ashoka. They came into the hall, and prostrated themselves in front of the statue of Lord Vishnu. They went to take 'theerth prasad' from the priest.

The priest looked at them and gave Rudra the first *theertham*. Rudra took it with great devotion. Moments later, he fell down, vomiting blood.

The boys shouted. The priest was bewildered. Hearing

their shouts, Acharya rushed in. They tried to revive Rudra.

But Rudra's soul had departed from his body.

Acharya could not control his emotions.'Who can erase what the creator has inscribed upon our foreheads at the time of birth? Many astrologers warned that Rudra would face fatal danger at the age of thirty. We could not stop this! Rudra, God is not present in the idols. Your feelings are our God. Your soul is our God. Who killed you?'

Samrat Chandragupta and Queen Helen came to pay their last respects to Rudra.

Acharya Chanakya regained his composure a few hours later. He ordered the arrest of the priest whose holy water had killed Rudra. He addressed the huge crowd that had assembled. 'Fellow countrymen, the sacred *theertham* gives purity after prolonged contact, but a darshan of the great son of our empire has the ability to purify one immediately. Have a darshan of Rudra for the last time and pay homage to him.

'The fragrance of flowers spreads only in the direction of the wind. But the goodness of Rudra spreads in all directions. He was a man who was great because of his deeds, not his birth. Good men like Rudra are rarely isolated peaks; they are the summits of ranges.

'Rudra, to the world you may be one person, but to me you are the world.' With tears rolling from his eyes, Acharya Chanakya closed the eyes of his last student, Rudra,

Rudra's body was cremated with full royal honours. A state mourning was declared for seven days. But who had killed Rudra, and why?

85

The royal court assembled. Samrat Chandragupta and Acharya Chanakya were in the chair of judgement.

The priest was brought in.

'Did you give the *theertham* to Rudra?' Chanakya asked him.

'Yes.'

'Did it contain poison?'

'Yes.'

'Why did you give it to him?'

'I had been told to do so by Rudra.'

Those listening were shocked. 'What?' Acharya finally asked.

'Rudra came to me one week before the puja,' the priest explained. 'He asked me to give the poison mixed with holy water to Uranus Gupta and Ashoka. He wanted to destroy the lineage of Samrat Chandragupta. He told me to keep two vessels of holy water; one poisoned and the other pure.

'He asked me to give him the pure water first so that no one would suspect anything. After that, he wanted me to distribute the poisoned water to the royal princes. He threatened to kill my family if I did not follow his instructions. I simply obeyed his command with a twist. Instead of distributing poisoned water to the princes, I gave it to him.'

'How can we believe you?' Acharya thundered.

'Why should I lie? The same poison stock can be found in his house. He told me, he had enough poision to finish off the royal family, one by one.'

Chanakya ordered a search of Rudra's house. The soldiers found a sizeable quantity of the same poison that had killed him.

All the evidence seemed to tell against Rudra. He was about to be declared as an offender and a *desa drohi* posthumously. 'What a disgrace to a great warrior!' Chanakya could not believe what was going on. He shook his head, deciding that judgement would be reserved for the next day.

PART XII

The Turning Point

86

The court hearing resumed the next day. It was a full house. The council of ministers and many of the general public were present, as it was an important judgement.

'Rudra—is he a hero or villain?' That was the question in everyone's minds. All the evidence seemed to tell against him. But it was difficult to believe it. How could the man who had handed over his own father and brother to the Samrat turn out so?

Would the proceedings have gone differently had Rudra been alive?

Even Acharya Chanakya did not believe that Rudra could be a culprit. His intuition told him that his favourite student would not have been able to imagine such a heinous crime.

But sitting in the chair of a justice, he had to be dispassionate. He could not overrule evidence and judgements had to be based on what was before him. He could not show any bias in his judgement.

And now, the judgement was about to be delivered. Acharya Chanakya began reading the judgement written on the palm leaves.

Case 201/Karthika month/Manmadha varsha/Somavara/ panchami thithi.

Accused: Rudra (posthumous).

Crime: Attempt to destroy the royal lineage.

Since the accused is no more and cannot appear in person,

the judgement is delivered on the basis of evidence in front of us.

'Based on our hearings, Rudra is....'

Before Acharya could deliver the final word, there was a sudden commotion.

87

Uranus Gupta was brought in with blood all over his body. The whole darbar was stunned to see him.

Two security officials accompanied him as though he were the accused. There was pindrop silence in the darbar.

Acharya stopped reading. He asked the accompanying officials, 'What happened? Why is our royal prince Uranus Gupta here in this condition?'

'Sir, he murdered our queen just a few hours ago. We are guards from the queen's place.'

'What?' the whole darbar was shaken.

Acharya asked, 'Prince, did you murder your mother?'

'Yes, Acharya. Please hear me out. Last night I was listening to the conversation between my mother and the priest who was a witness in Rudra's case. My mother said to him, "Well done, priest. It is good that you did not fumble in court. The judgement against Rudra is certain. His name will always carry the stigma of a criminal in our history.

"'I came to this country not out of any sense of love. I wanted to complete the failed mission of Alexander and my father. I wanted to discover and pass on all the secrets regarding amrit and the Brahmastra. Whatever Rudra knew, he passed on to my son, as he held my son to be his foster son. I got all the secrets of various sciences through my Greek soldiers, who were married to the men of the Nava Yuva Sena. I came here with this hidden agenda and now my goal is fulfilled. I am now wrapping up my mission. Now I can make my son the next Samrat and pass on these sciences to Greece, my home."

"'Since you rendered great support to me in this, I will make you the chief priest of the empire and also the owner of ten villages."

"'Now Rudra will be declared a traitor, and there is no one to challenge me. For a while, he was suspicious about my declared intentions of adopting this land as my home. Now that he is finished, I can dominate the Rajneethi and influence the king. Only the old man Chanakya may create some troubles but he is old, and will soon die. Why should I commit an additional crime by murdering him? Thank you for completing this mission in a neat way without raising doubts in anyone's mind." The priest left happily.

'When I heard this, the blood boiled inside me, and I do not know what gave me strength. I took the knife and attacked my mother. She never expected it to come from me, and she could not defend herself. In a rage, I stabbed her all over her body, and she fell in a pool of blood.'

The court could not believe what that young boy had said.

88

'Can we consider a child of five years an accused? Or can we consider him as a witness?' one of the ministers asked.

Samrat had not come out of the shock yet. It was a double blow for him: his friend Rudra was gone, now his lover, Queen Helen, was gone. What was left for him?

Acharya Chanakya intervened. 'Evidence in any form is acceptable, since Rudra is not alive to defend himself. Age is not the criterion for authenticity. Further, the prince has killed his own mother in a rage. This is not an ordinary murder. We should consider him an authentic and valid witness in this case.

'Now we must summon the priest.'

The priest was cross-examined and he accepted the story Uranus Gupta had narrated. But the priest also said that the poison powder had been delivered through Visaka, the blind brother-in-law of Rudra. Visaka was summoned.

'I have been worrying about the threat to Rudra's life. Since my Greek wife also knows this, Queen Helen might have learned it from her. Queen Helen told me that special prayers were arranged in the temple for Rudra. She gave me some powder packets and asked me to hand them over to the priest. I gave him one, and left the rest in Rudra's house, where I also stay. I was told that these packets contained "prashad" blessed to ensure the longevity of Rudra. I did not know what was inside those packets. I did not open them.

'Looking back now, I realize I was used as a messenger to

go between Queen Helen and the priest. This must have been done to protect the priest. Had his story not been accepted for some reason, my story would have strengthened the case against Rudra. But the turn of events did not give room for this. That is all I know. I do not have any further role in this matter.'

The priest was jailed. Queen Helen was cremated. Her son and killer Uranus Gupta performed the last rites for his mother. Rudra was posthumously cleared of all accusations.

The next day, Samrat Chandragupta convened a condolence and appreciation meeting for Rudra. All his ministers were present.

Acharya Chanakya paid tribute to Rudra.

'The fragrance of flowers spreads only in the direction of the wind. But the goodness of Rudra spreads in all directions. The earth is scented by a flower that falls upon it, but the flower does not collect the odour of the earth. Rudra is a flower; he only spread good things around him.

'It is a passion and not the position you hold that will lead to success. Rudra pursued with passion the rendering of unceasing service to his land without looking at the size of the rewards.

'I will miss him forever. He will forever live in our minds, even though he has gone far away! May his soul rest in peace!'

Samrat took his turn. 'The trouble started with the non-acceptance of good in others. If we accept that good, it becomes an inspiration. Rudra is an inspiration; Helen was envious since she did not accept his good. If she had accepted him as the good person as he was, it would have become an unconditional love. Her resistance created stress. That is her fate. The hearts of the average person burn in the fire of other's fame and they slander them. Helen was an average woman who suffered from her jealousy. Jealousy is the tribute mediocrity pays to genius.

'Sacrifice is the passion of great souls, but never the law of societies. Rudra was a great soul; he breathed sacrifice till the end. He gave me his unstinting support right from the age of three. The wars we won, the empire we built, the impregnable safety around me—all are due to him. I credit this whole empire to Rudra's work. His inspiration and perspiration have together produced a sensation that is so powerful that it is beyond measurement.

'Apart from his lifelong service to the nation, he gave a parting gift to me in the form of imparting his knowledge to my proud little prince, Uranus Gupta, whom he considered his foster son. The little prince has stepped into the shoes of his foster father in his dedication and unshakable regard for his duty.

'Unless a kernel of wheat falls to the ground and dies, it remains only a single seed. But if it does fall, produces many seeds. The mother seed of the Mauryan empire was sown into our soil and will give birth to so many patriotic sons like Uranus Gupta in the years ahead! May God bless our realm.

'Having lost my love and my life, I am shattered. Very soon, I will be moving south, relinquishing my material life. Bindusara will take over after me. Along with Acharya, and the able council of ministers, he will continue to govern the realm.'

The whole hall was emotional. No one uttered a single word. They were shaken by the turn of events.

Swastika, Rudra's wife, concluded the session. 'I have no interest in life after Rudra's untimely death. But I will live with the memories of him and help to bring up his foster son, Uranus Gupta. I will bring him up as a true warrior, just like his foster father, Rudra.' Tears were rolling down from her eyes.

Epilogue

Twenty-five years later

There was a fire raging within the chamber. Uranus Gupta, and Ashoka were shouting from outside.

'Acharya, please do not immolate yourself. We need your guidance. Please do not leave us alone. Please come out before the fire spreads...'

Acharya shouted back. 'Princes, listen to me. One of the most effective ways to kill a king is to poison him. To ensure that our king would not be affected by poison, I built up Chandragupta's immunity. To do this, unknown to the king, I would mix a very small amount of poison in his food. When Queen Durdhara was heavily pregnant, she mistakenly consumed the poisoned food meant for her husband. She collapsed and I was called in. Upon understanding the situation, there were two choices, to save the mother with the antidote, or the child.

'I gave prominence to the continuity of the lineage rather than the mother's life. The son was taken from his mother's womb in the nick of time. The poison and the cutting of her womb led to the queen's death. Just a bit of the poison reached the boy and he was marked with a blue-tinged dot or bindu. This was the origin of the name Bindusara, who is our current emperor and successor of Samrat Chandragupta.

The story of his birth was kept secret from him. He did not know how his mother died.

'Bindusara ascended the throne, and I continued to advise him but the other advisor, Subandhu, wanted the ear of the emperor all to himself. He gave a perverted version of the story of the emperor's birth and blamed me for the death of his mother. As a consequence, Bindusara sidelined me. The respect his father showed me is now history. Subandhu and the council of ministers keep reminding Bindusara that I am the killer of his mother.

'Rather than facing the ignominy of my diminished stature, I choose to end my life. I will immolate myself on a heap of dung cakes in my own chambers. I lived my life on my own terms, challenging mighty empires. The world will laugh at me for this step I am taking. But I do not want the Mauryan empire, which I built with my sweat, to take a wrong decision and mark me as guilty. Bindusara is not Chandragupta. He is heavily influenced by others, unlike his father who listened to everyone but ultimately made his own decisions. It is better for me to carry the stigma of suicidal death rather than my emperor bearing the guilt of a wrong judgement. Hence, I have decided to move away from this world. The suicide is not an act of cowardice but an act triggered by unshakable love for the Mauryan empire.

'Uranus Gupta, you are the prodigy of Rudra. I ask of you one favour. Never ever let the nine secret *shastras* reach the hands of alien invaders. If found necessary, hide these *shastras* from the public forever to avoid bringing disaster to humanity. You are now the chief protector of these *shastras*. You have a great responsibility, my dear prince. Do not bother about me, since my mission is over. I am now moving away from this world. Support Ashoka in consolidating the Mauryan empire once he becomes the ruler! Goodbye!'

He recited the famous prayer....

Asato ma sat gamaya
Tamaso ma jyotir gamaya
Mrityor ma amritam gamaya

(Lead us, Oh Lord, from Untruth to Truth,
Lead us, Oh Lord, from Darkness to Light,
Lead us, Oh Lord, from Death to Life)

May the holy land of Bharat,
Guarded by the mountains and the sea,
Never stray from the path of dharma,
Whatever her future fate may be...

Uranus Gupta wanted to stop him. King Bindusara realized his mistake and tried to join the princes, but it was too late. The Acharya had resolved to die.

In the end, Chanakya's death was as spectacular as his life. He lit his own pyre and died in a roaring fireball. He chose to face his creator in death just as he had faced the world in his life, on his own terms and at a time of his choosing.

The Kalinga War

Kalinga, once under Magadha rule, regained its independence shortly after Chandragupta consolidated his rule. Chandragupta and Bindusara, the first two Mauryan emperors, did not think of invading the strong kingdom. The third Mauryan emperor, Ashoka, took it upon himself to undertake that invasion. Uranus Gupta supported him. With all the secret sciences under his command and with the able assistance of the Nava

Yuva Sena under the captaincy of Uranus Gupta, Kalinga was plundered and destroyed. More than 100,000 people were killed.

After the war, a few women approached Emperor Ashoka and said, 'Your actions have taken my father, husband and son. Now what do I have to live for?'

Moved by these words and the fear that humanity would be destroyed if the nine secret sciences were left open, Ashoka and Uranus Gupta decided to exit the *shastras*.

The Rudrakshas and the palm leaves with the secret sciences were buried below the sanctum sanctorum of the various temples in the eight directions of north, south, east and west. This was done to enable them to guard the land from invasion and also to avoid letting these precious sciences fall into the wrong hands.

The names of temples where they were buried were kept confidential, and interred in the souls of nine men, who were not visible to humanity. Perhaps these shastras may be lying buried below the sanctum sanatorum of one of the temples in modern India today.

The clan of Rudra Sena, whose mantle was inherited by Uranus Gupta, now guard these temples. Where are these nine unknown men? When will they assemble again?

The Nine secret sciences may be in any of these confidential locations.

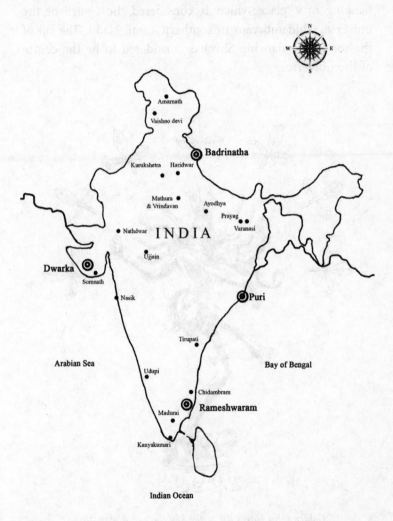

Map: Not to scale. The international boundaries on the map are neither purported to be correct nor authentic by Survey of India directives.

It is rumoured that the golden bilva leaves can be found hanging in a place which is considered the centre of the universe, Chidambaram in southern Tamil Nadu. The tip of the toe of the dancing Shiva is considered to be the centre of the universe.

Golden bilva leaves led to the key clues of Brahmastra.

A curtain can be found within the sanctum sanctorum, the drawing of which reveals an empty space with streams of golden bilva leaves hanging to indicate the presence of the Lord. It is called the 'Chidambara Rahasyam' and considered to indicate the journey from ignorance to wisdom. The clues to the Brahmastra lie here as silent golden leaves, which will be activated only when all the nine sciences are assembled! Perhaps this will only happen when the nine men assemble at the birth of the last avatar of Lord Vishnu, when Kalki arrives heralded by the Chiranjivis.

A new karmic journey was waiting for Rudra, the hero who never worried about fame, name or kingdom and rendered unselfish service to his land. Rudra, the man who protected the emperor and his sons and was killed by poison mixed with sacred water at a temple. The same sacred water that killed him welcomed him at his birth in his next karmic outing. The same water that had killed him made him extraordinarily proficient in the maritime wars that took place during his next karmic journey, when he returned as a commander for Rajendra Chola.

Rudra's second karmic journey will be revealed in the upcoming book of this series:

The Conquest of the East [Janam Three]

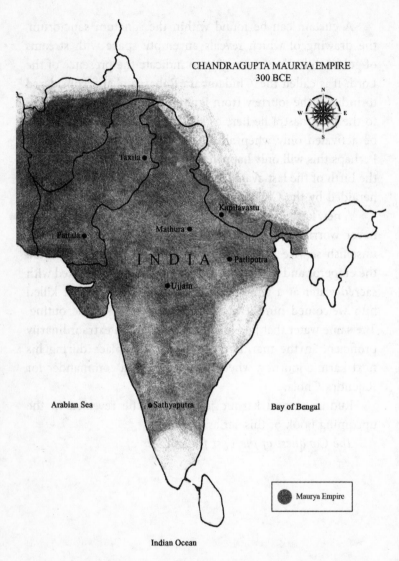

CHANDRAGUPTA MAURYA EMPIRE
300 BCE

Taxila

Kapilavastu

Pattala

Mathura

Patliputra

INDIA

Ujjain

Arabian Sea

Sathyaputra

Bay of Bengal

Maurya Empire

Indian Ocean

Map: Not to scale. The international boundaries on the map are neither purported to be correct nor authentic by Survey of India directives.

Acknowledgements

At the outset, I have to thank the Almighty for kindling my passion to write fiction. This thought came from nowhere and I trace it to divine directions. What did not occur to me in the last four decades suddenly arose in my mind as a spark one fine morning. This spark has lit flames of unbridled passion in me.

I register my gratitude to my think tank. Its members tolerated my constant intrusion into their personal time. They supported me in terms of perfecting the core story, ensuring the smooth flow of the narrative and the promotional aspects of the book. The key members of this think tank, who walked along with me shoulder to shoulder on this project, are: Padmanabh Diwanji (or Paddy) from the UAE, Priyanka Durgadoss and Jyothsna Durgadoss from California, USA.

There was a supporting think tank that relentlessly assisted me in terms of the research, conversion of manuscripts into digital files and taking on the role of critics. They are Chandramouli Raman (USA), Shyaam Nagarajan (USA), Tarannum Malik (UAE) and Vijayakumaran (UAE). I should also acknowledge Ravi Krishnaswamy (India) who assisted me with the Sanskrit translations in this book.

I am grateful to my publishers, Rupa Publications India Pvt. Ltd and Kapish Mehra, Managing Director, Rupa Publications, for showing confidence in this book, from its inception to its completion. The assistance we got from Dibakar Ghosh,

Editorial Director and Legal Head was invaluable. Dibakar and his editorial team have provided valuable editorial inputs to improve the book. I would like to register my gratitude to Madhav Menon (UAE) whose enthusiastic guidance from day one helped convert my dream into reality. In addition to serving as an advisory board member on this project along with Padmanabh Diwanji, he was also instrumental in helping me reach the right publisher.

Above all, I could not have spent quality time on this project, but for the support of my wife Gowri Durgadoss. In addition, I owe my gratitude to Suresh Bhatia and Rajeev Bhatia (UAE), the businessmen who support me in every one of my projects.

Further, I thank all my well-wishers who follow my Facebook pages, Twitter, YouTube, Google Plus, my blogs and my author website.

This book relies on a vast body of research and artistic work by a number of scholars—numerous books, various articles, journals and websites. I thank all these sources and have cited them wherever possible.

Finally, since I am not able to individually thank all my well-wishers, I register my debt of gratitude to all of them collectively.

Glossary

Aindra—Entry.

Amrit—The elixir of life. Also means nectar; mythical drink which grants the drinker eternal life. It is sometimes equated with philosopher's stones. Alchemists in various ages and cultures sought the meaning of formulating the elixir of life.

Anahata—Unstruck sound (the sound of the celestial realm).

Ashuras—In Indian mythology it means a class of divine beings representing 'evil'.

Astra—Missile.

Athithi Devo Bhava—Guests are equivalent to God.

Balir Vyaso Hanumanshcha Vibhishanaha Krupaha Parashuramasaha Saptaitey Chiranjivaha—Ashwathama, King Mahabali, Vyasa, Hanuman, Vibishan, Kripacharya and Parashuram are the seven death-defying or imperishable personalities.

Bharat Aur Yavanas Ki Jaya Ho—Bharat and Greeks are victorious.

Bindi—A decorative dot or mark worn in the middle of the forehead by Indian women, especially Hindus.

Bhoomi putra—The son of earth.

Brahmastra—The mythical weapon that can cause the destruction of the humanity.

Chidambara Rahasyam—The secret of Chidambaram, the temple town of south India.

Chiranjivis—Immortal living beings, according to Hinduism.

Cuckoos—A greyish bird.

Darbha—A grass blade.

Desa Drohi—Traitor to the motherland or one's own country.

Dhams—Abodes/Seats. Four dhams revered by Hindus are Badrinath, Dwarka, Puri and Rameswaram.

Ejat—Exit.

Jal Samadhi—Grave in water.

Janma—Birth.

Jaya Ho—Victorious

Kali Yuga—The last of the four yugas with 432,000 years. The other yugas are the Satya, Treta and Dvapara Yugas.

Kalki—Tenth and last incarnation of Lord Vishnu who is yet to come to this world.

Karma Yogi—A person who is focused on his duties.

Karmic—Action, seen as bringing upon oneself inevitable results, good or bad, either in this life or in a reincarnation—(beliefs of Hinduism/Buddhism).

Meri Raksha Karo—Save me.

Mizithra Cheese—'Mizithra' is a Greek word. It means fresh cheese made with milk and whey from sheep and or goats. The ratio of milk to whey usually is 7:3. It resembles Italian ricotta through mizithra is typically drier.

Mudhra—*Seal*—In those days the kingdom endorsed its authorization through seals.

Nadis—Pulse.

Navaratri—The nine days of celebration of the Hindus dedicated to the goddess, Durga.

Om, Tryambakam yajamahe sugandhim pushti-vardhanam Urvarukamiva bandhanan Mrityor mukshiya mamritat—This is called the Mritunjaya mantra. It is a prayer to Lord Shiva for liberation from death.

Paksha—In Sanskrit, it refers to a fortnight.

Parampara—The succession from Guru to disciple, a tradition handed down through ages.

Pithaji—A form of addressing one's father with respect.

Puranas—Ancient mythological treatises.

Raja Seleukos Ki Jaya Ho—Raja Seleukos is victorious.

Rajaguru—The Royal advisor to the king.

Rajaneethi—The royal justice.

Rakshas—A spiritual wristband usually worn as a symbol to protect the wearer from evil.

Sadhus—Saints.

Samudra—Ocean.

Sanatana Dharma—The eternal law of the cosmos according to Hinduism.

Satya—One of the four yugas.

Shivratri—The Hindu festival celebrated annually in reverence to Lord Shiva.

Siddhi—Enlightenment.

Suvarnas—Golden coins.

Theerth prasad—The sacred water to be consumed as God's blessed gift.

Theerthams—Location of sacred water.

Tishya—Auspicious.

Varnas—The four divisions of Vedic society—Brahmins, Kshatriyas, Vaisyas and Shudras.

Vimana—Aeroplane.

Vrata Kshatriya—Brave member of the second highest of the four varnas (castes) of traditional Indian society. They are responsible for upholding and justice, social harmony, governance, including defence and law and order.

Yachak—A begger/person looking for alms.

Yadava—A community that is believed to descend from the mythical King 'Yadu.' They worship Lord Krishna, who also came from the community.

Yagna—It is a ritual of Hindus, while praying.

Yuga Purush—Personality of a yuga.

Yuga—The time scale of the universe measured through this term.

Bibliography

Books

'Alexander the Great, a Biography,' Shree Book Centre.

'Chandragupta Maurya,' Series—Indian Mythology & Tales/History/Divinity—Vol. MITD.001, Wilco Publishing House, 2011.

Barat, Dr Pradip K., 'National Identity & Heritage of India,' Star Publishing, Canada, 2010.

Bhargava, Purushottam Lal Bhargava, *Chandragupta Maurya*, The Upper India Publishing House Ltd, Lucknow, 1935.

Das, P.K., 'Unparalled Diplomat Chanakya,' Mahaveer Publishers, Delhi, 2012.

Deshpande G.P., 'Chanakya Vishnugupta,' Seagull Books, Calcutta, 1996.

Gavin, Tamila, 'Alexander the Great, Man, Myth or Monster?, Walker Books, London 2011.

Lonsdale, David 'Alexander the Great—Lessons in Strategy,' Routlege, Taylor & Francis Group, London and New York, 2007.

Mukherjee, Radha Kumud, 'Chandragupta Maurya and His Times,' Madras University Sir William Meyer Lecturer, 1940–41, Motilal Banarsidass Publishers (Pvt) Ltd, New Delhi.

Pattanaik, Devdutt '7 Secrets of Vishnu,' Westland, Delhi, 2011.

Rao, Subba, 'Chandragupta Maurya, the Determined Prince,' Scripter, Amar Chitra Katha (Pvt) Ltd, Mumbai, 1978.

Romm, James 'Ghost on the Throne,' Alfred A. Knopf, New York, 2011.

Sameer, M.A., 'Emperor Chandragupta Maurya,' Scripter, Manoj Publications, Delhi.

Sharma, Yagya, 'Chanakya, the King Maker, Scripter, Amar Chitra Katha (Pvt) Ltd, Mumbai, 1971.

Visakhadatta 'Mudrarakshasa,' Tukaram Javaji, Bombay, 1893.

Yenne, Bill, 'Alexander the Great, Palgrave Macmillan, 2010.

Web Archives (Accessed on 5 May 2016):

http://family.wikinut.com/An-Indo-Greek -Love Affair/z4f9u5kg/

http://spokensanskrit.de/indexphp?tinput=ziro&direction=SE&script=Hk&link=yes&beginning=0

http://hindumyths.blogspot.com/2008/05/eight-chiranjeevis-part-0.html

https://www.quora.com/What-happened-after-the-Mahabharat-war

www.hindu-mythology.faithweb.com/index_12.html

http://in.lifestyle.yahoo.com/photos/dhanushkodi-at-land-s-end-slideshow/dhanushkodi-photo-1338448880.html

www.hinduwisdom.info/articles_hinduism/246.htm

http://larryavisbrown.homestead.com/files/xeno.mahabcomm.htm

http://en.wikipedia.org/wiki/Mudrarakshasa

http://en.wikipedia.org/wiki/Chittorgarh_Fort

http://en.wikipedia.org/wiki/Physical_attractiveness

http://answers.yahoo.com/question/index?qid=20090905025447AA5ZFSK

http://descriptivewriting.wordpass.com/tag/describing-handsome-men/

http://descriptivewriting.wordpress.com/2012/11/22/describing-a-beautiful-woman-2/

http://en.wikipedia.org/wiki/Physical_attractiveness

http://descriptivewriting.wordpress.com/tag/describing-handsome-men/

http://descritivewriting.wordpress.com/2012/11/22/describing-a -beautiful-woman-2

http://bje117.hubpages.com/hub/talldarkandhandsome

http://www.khandro.net/nature_mountain.htm

http://www.yogamag.net/archives/1979/emay79/glimpses.shtml

http://omshivam.wordpress.com/vedic-astrology-jyothish-light-of-knowledge/maha-kumbha/a-journey-to-kailas-mansarovar/the-mystery-of-holy-kailash-manasaras/

http://en.wikipedia.org/wiki/indus_Valley_Civilization

www.kidsgen.com/fables_and_fairytales/indian_mythology_stories/arjunas_search.htm

http://chandrakantmarwadi.com/myth-news/armrut-ghat-holy-grail-will-satyuga-come-back/

www.paralumun.com/numerology.htm

http://hans.wyrdweb.eu/tag/magic-square/

http://en.wikipedia.org/wiki/Alchemy

www.hinduwebsite.com/numbers.asp

http://www.ridingthebeast.com/numbers/nu22.php

http://wikipedia.org/wiki/Ujjain http://www.google.co.in/earch?q=indus+ valley+script+symbols&sa=X&tbm=isch&tbo=u& source=univ&ei=h7pEU4L CoSqhAffsIGIBw&ved=0CDAQ7Ak&biw=

http://www.deccanherald.com/content/19758/cracking-indus-valley-script.html

http://www.readindus.com/

http://www.sci-news.com/othersciences/linguistics/science-indus-script-sanskrit-language-01777.html

http://www.princeton.edu/

http://en.wikipedia.org/wiki/Ashwatthama

http://family.wikinut.com/An-Indo-Greek-Love-Affair/z4f9u5kg/

http://indiaopines.com/chandra-gupta-maurya-greek-princess-helen-love-story/

http://en.wikipedia.org/wiki/Seleucus_I_Nicator#chandragupta_and_the_eastern_provineces

http://guides.wikinut.com/Seleucus-was-defeated-by-chandragupta-Maurya/1zc3jy_h/

http://experiencehinduism.com/interesting-stories/heracles-derived-from-krishna

http://www.pantheon.org/articles/a/apollo.html

www.livius.org/aj-al/alexander/alexander13.html

http://en.wikipedia.org/wiki/indian_campaign_of_Alexander_the_Great

http://maddy06.blogspot.ae/2008/10/roxane-and-rakhi.html

http://historicalleys.blogspot.ae/2009/02/calanus-and-alexander.html

www.livius.org/caa-can/calanus/calanus.html

http://archives.mirroroftomorrow.org/blog/_archives/2010/4/22/4501082.html

http://en.wikipedia.org/wiki/taxiles
http://en.wikipedia.org/wiki/Battle_of_the_Hydaspes
http://virajgupta.blogspot.com/2008/05/mystery-of-floating-stones.html
http://kumbh-mela.euttaranchal.com/history-kumbh-mela.php
http://en.wikipedia.org/wiki/Haridwar
http://en.wikipedia.org/wiki/Ramanathaswamy_Temple
http://en.wikipedia.org/wiki/Dhanushkodi
www.sawaal.ibibo.com/puja-and-rituals/what-theerthams-inside-
rameswaram-temple-tamilnadu-488909.html
http://www.astroved.com/blogs/chidambaram-rahasyam-the-
chidambaram-temple-secret
http://hinduism.about.com/od/basics/a/monthsdayseras.htm
www.sushmajee.com/information/sites-videos/chandragupta/95-97-tv-
chandragupt.htm
http://answers.yahoo.com/question/index?qid=20101017053445AA9wtcR
https://Ivnaga.wordpress.com/2014/01/28/ancient-mystery-thriller/
http://hinduism.iskcon.org/practice/503.htm
http://www.historydiscussion.net/history-of-india/what-are-the-causes-of-
the-kalinga-war/2415
http://en.m.wikipedia.org/wiki/Kalinga_War
http://historyofindia-madhunimkar.blogspot.ae/2009/09/kingdom-of-
maurya.html?m=1
http://en.m.wikipedia.org/wiki/Conquest_of_Nanda_Empire
http://en.wikipedia.org/wiki/Elixir_or_life
http://en.wikipedia.org/wiki/Ambrosia
http://kumbh-mela.euttaranchal.com/history-kumbha-mela.php
http://hans.wyrdweb.eu/tag/magic-square/
http://ignca.nic.in/ps_04014.htm
http://www.hindunet.org/srh_home/1996_2/msg00272.html
www.indiadivine.org/audarya/hinduism-forum/415261-sri-markandeya-
ancient-hindu-rishi.html
http://en.wikipedia.org/wiki/Har_ki_Pauri
http://en.wikipedia.org/wiki/Ujjain
http://en.wikipedia.org/wiki/Panch_Prayag

http://sacredsites.com/asia/india/shiva_shrines.html

http://hindustories.blogspot.ae/2012_06_01_archive.html

http://spiritualsoul.net/profiles/blogs/significance-of-number-8-in-hinduism

http://www.macmillandictionary.com/thesaurus-category/british/Easy-to-trick-or-deceive

www.1stmuse.com/frames/sasigupta.html

http://varnam.nationalinterest.in/2010/04/takshashila-2-kings-a-king-maker-2/

http://aumamen.com/topic/ashta-siddhis-other-supernatural-powers

http://www.beliefnet.com/Faiths/Hinduism/Articles/Ashta-Siddhis-Are-Recipes-For-Success-Without-Stress.aspx

http://projectavalon.net/forum4/showthread.php?50876-The-Mysterious-Last-Door-At-Padmanabhaswamy-Temple-Breaking-News

www.numerology-thenumbersandtheirmeanings.blogspot.ae/2011/05/number-22.html

www.magic-squares.net/premeter.htm

https://sites.google.com/site/indusharappacivilization/indus-dictionary

http://www.sci-news.com/othersciences/linguistics/science-indus-sanskrit-language-01777.html

http://www.harappa.com/script/diction.html

https://sites.google.com/site/indusharappacivilization/2-indus-dictionary--words

http://hans.wyrdweb.eu/tag/magic-square/

www.hinduwebsite.com/numbers.asp

http://www.comparativereligion.com/avatars.html

http://ancientindians.wordpress.com/2009/09/24/the-avatars-of-vishnu/

http://www.ridingthebeast.com/numbers/nu22.php

http://mathforum.org/library/drmath/view/56857.html

www.lib.usm.edu/spcol/exhibitions/item_of_the_month/iotm_nov_08.html

http://en.wikipedia.org/wiki/Palm-leaf_manuscript

http://projectavalon.net/forum4/showthread.php?50876-The-Mysterious-Last-Door-At-Padmanabhaswamy-Temple-Breaking-News

www.thelivingmoon.com/43ancients/02files/India_Ancient_City_

Rajasthan_near_Jodhpurt.html
www.rinkworks.com/words/palindromes.shtml
www.stotrapushpalu.blogspot.com/2012/04/7-chiranjeevis-seven-chirnjeevis-in.html
www.india-forums.com/forum_posts.asp?TID=2926200&tpn=3
http://in.answers.yahoo.com/question/index?qid=20111219055744AA0PujE
http://www.saicast.org/documentaries/secretcave.html
http://www.theholidayspot.com/kumbh_mela/maha_kumbh_mela.htm
www.yatra2yatra.com/hinduism/mahakumbh
http://en.wikipedia.org/wiki/Triveni_Sangam
www.journey2light.wordpress.com/2013/01/04/indias-kumbh-mela-its-mythological-story/
http://en.wikipedia.org/wiki/Samudra_manthan
http://en.wikipedia.org/wiki/Sarayu
https://en.m.wikipedia.org/wiki/Rudraksha
https://en.m.wikipedia.org/wiki/Rudraksha
https://en.wikipedia.org/wiki/Amrita
www.theindianmythology.wordpress.com/tag/rishi-markandeya/
http://en.wikipedia.org/wiki/Faizabad
http://www.valmikiramayan.net/bala/sarga24/bala_24_prose.htm
http://www.indianetzone.com/46/last_days_rama.htm
https://www.quora.com/How-did-Lord-Rama-attain-his-death-or-end-his-form-avatar
www.knowswhy.com/why-is-kripacharya-immortal/
https://in.answers.yahoo.com/question/index?qid=20110915061759AAMGgl
https://thekarna.wordpress.com/2010/05/12/ashwatthama-the-12th-rudra/
www.dilipkumar.in/travel/piligrim/jyotirlingas/ramesh.php
http://lordrama.co.in/shri-ramsetu.html
http://www.mallstuffs.com/Blogs/BlogDetails.aspx?BlogId=249&BlogType=Spiritual&Topic=Why%20scientists%20want%20to%20protect%20ram%20setu
www.socialcause.org/getarticlefromdb.php?id=1368
http://ramasetu.blogspot.ae/2007/03/setu-in-mahabharat.html

www.chillibreeze.com/articles_various/Rameswaram.asp
www.sarojbala.blogspot.ae
www.adhyatmikasampada.blogspot.ae/2010/02/14-understanding-
brahmastra-physical.html
www.troolyunbelievable.blogspot.ae/2007/07/oldest-secret-society-on-
earth.html
http://www.beliefnet.com/Faiths/Hinduism/Articles/Ashta-Siddhis-Are-
Recipes-For-Success-Without-Stress.aspx
http://aumamen.com/topic/ashta-siddhis-other-supernatural-powers
http://en.wikipedia.org/wiki/Siddhi#Eight_pri_siddhis
www.indohistory.com/nine_unknown_men.html
http://en.wikipedia.org/wiki/Alchemy
www.ivarta.com/columns/OL_050307.htm
www.spokensanskrit.de/index.php?script=HK&beginning=0+&tinput=
+Mineral&trans=Translate&direction=ES
https://ramanan50.wordpress.com/2014/06/04/brahmastra-invocation-
mantra-other-astras/